MW01040359

RACHMANINOFF

SELECTED WORKS FOR THE PIANO

EDITED BY MURRAY BAYLOR

Alfred has made every effort to make this book not only attractive but more useful and long-lasting as well. Usually, large books do not lie flat or stay open on the music rack. In addition, the pages (which are glued together) tend to break away from the spine after repeated use.

In this edition, pages are sewn together in multiples of 16. This special process prevents pages from falling out of the book while allowing it to stay open for ease in playing. We hope this unique binding will give you added pleasure and additional use.

Second Edition

Copyright © MCMXCIII by Alfred Publishing Co., Inc.
All rights reserved.   Printed in USA.

Cover art: A detail from Cupolas and Swallows
by Juon Konstantin (1875–1958)
Tretjakov Gallery, Moscow
Art Resource, New York

CONTENTS

Foreword ... 2
The Man ... 2
The Music ... 4
This Anthology ... 5
General Suggestions ... 6
The Pieces ... 6
Recommended Reading ... 113
Recommended Listening ... 113
Prelude in C-sharp Minor, Op. 3, No. 2 ... 11
Polichinelle in F-sharp Minor, Op. 3, No. 4 ... 17
Sérénade in B-flat Minor, Op. 3, No. 5 ... 27
Barcarolle in G Minor, Op. 10, No. 3 ... 32
Mélodie in E Minor, Op. 10, No. 4 ... 44
Humoresque in G, Op. 10, No. 5 ... 50
Moment Musical in D-flat, Op. 16, No. 5 ... 59
Prelude in D, Op. 23, No. 4 ... 64
Prelude in G Minor, Op. 23, No. 5 ... 69
Prelude in E-flat, Op. 23, No. 6 ... 77
Prelude in G-flat, Op. 23, No. 10 ... 82
Prelude in B-flat Minor, Op. 32, No. 2 ... 84
Prelude in G, Op. 32, No. 5 ... 90
Prelude in F, Op. 32, No. 7 ... 95
Prelude in B Minor, Op. 32, No. 10 ... 99
Prelude in B, Op. 32, No. 11 ... 104
Etude-Tableau in G Minor, Op. 33, No. 8 ... 108

SERGEI VASILYEVICH RACHMANINOFF

(April 2, 1873 — March 21, 1943)

FOREWORD

THE MAN

Rachmaninoff was born in the Novgorod district of Russia in 1873, the year that Debussy became 10 years old and Liszt 61. Both his father and mother belonged to the upper class of Russian society and had inherited large holdings of land. The father, a military officer, was a charming person—warm and loving toward his children but addicted to gambling and riotous living. The mother, a rather stern person, seemed to do her duty somewhat coldly by her six children. The father's behavior eventually caused the ruin of the family fortune, and Rachmaninoff's parents had to sell their last estate and move to St. Petersburg (now Leningrad) the year that Sergei was nine years old—in 1882. A short time later the parents separated, the children staying with their mother.

The boy's extraordinary musical gifts had already been discovered and encouraged by good training, so that he received a scholarship at the St. Petersburg Conservatory shortly after the family moved to that city. Unfortunately his motivation at that time didn't match his talent, and he failed to take his work very seriously. His mother, concerned about his further education, consulted his older cousin, Alexander Siloti, who had just returned from a period of study with Liszt and was beginning his career as a piano virtuoso. Siloti said that he would recommend the boy to Nicolai Zverev, who had been his own teacher, and urged the mother to send her son to Moscow to work under the strict discipline of Zverev, who taught gifted young pianists in the lower levels of instruction at the Moscow Conservatory. A few students lived in Zverev's home, had their lessons there, and had their practice supervised by the professor and his sister. Rachmaninoff went to the Zverev house in the fall of 1885, when he was 12, and lived and studied there for four years. While under Zverev's tutelage he not only developed his pianistic ability through expert training and well-directed practice, but he also heard the extraordinary series of historical recitals of keyboard music given by Anton Rubenstein and became acquainted with many important Russian musicians, among them Tchaikowsky. When Rachmaninoff left the Zverev house and entered the upper level courses at the Moscow Conservatory he studied piano with Siloti, counterpoint with Taniev, and composition with Arensky in a class that included Alexander Scriabin. Rachmaninoff graduated from the conservatory a year earlier than most students—at the age of 19—and was given a rarely awarded "great gold medal" of the conservatory, having finished with highest honors in both piano and composition.

From his early maturity to the middle of his life Rachmaninoff had a variety of experiences as a free artist, making the best of opportunities, and struggling with personal problems. His music was published almost as soon as he graduated from the conservatory, partly on the strength of Tchaikowsky's enthusiasm for it, and he continued to compose while earning a rather insecure living as accompanist, piano soloist, and conductor. His one-act opera *Aleko*, written as a final examination in composition at the conservatory, was produced by the Bolshoi Opera in 1893 and was praised by Tchaikowsky who heard the first performance. The friendship and encouragement of the older man meant a great deal to the 20-year-old Rachmaninoff, but the premiere of his opera was little more than six months past when Tchaikowsky died at the age of 53.

In 1895 Rachmaninoff started to compose his first symphony, a work he hoped would enhance his growing reputation, but when the symphony was played for the first time in 1897 in St. Petersburg the critics were merciless. They didn't realize that, in part, their impression of the work was a result of inadequate rehearsal and a poor performance. Rachmaninoff was so discouraged by this fiasco that he was depressed for months. He refused to have the work repeated under more favorable circumstances; indeed it was never played again during his lifetime. Though his fame was growing, and he was invited to London to play and conduct his music, he continued to brood over the disastrous premiere of his first large work for orchestra alone. He had begun to work on his second piano concerto, scheduled for a first performance in London the following season, but had reached an impasse and found himself unable to continue an excellent beginning. A friend suggested he consult Dr. Nicolai Dahl, a physician and amateur musician who had treated emotional illness successfully with suggestion and hypnosis. He began to see Dr. Dahl daily in January of 1900. A few months later his artistic impotence was cured, and he was able to finish the ever-popular C minor concerto which he dedicated to Dr. Dahl.

The year 1902 marked a major change in his life because in that year, when he was 29, he married his cousin, Natalya Satina. A year later their first daughter was born. He conducted at the Bolshoi Opera from 1904 to 1906 while working on two operas of his own, but unsatisfactory production conditions at the opera house and the political unrest following the 1905 revolution led him to move with his family to Dresden where he was better able to work on new compositions. In 1909 he came to the United States to play and conduct his music, particularly the new third piano concerto which he played with the New York Philharmonic Orchestra under Walter Damrosch. While in the United States he was offered the conductorship of the Boston Symphony Orchestra which had become vacant, but he refused. After his experience in the United States he returned to Russia to continue conducting, visited England again to play and conduct, and had a brief stay in Rome in 1913. In spite of the advantages of living in Germany or Italy the Rachmaninoffs preferred to make their home in Russia.

The Russian revolution of 1917 led to the greatest change of all in the life of the Rachmaninoff family. They were in Russia at the time of the Czar's abdication and the resulting political upheavals. While the turmoil was at its height, Rachmaninoff received an invitation to play recitals in Sweden, with the likelihood of repeating them in other Scandinavian countries. Unsure of what the future might hold in Russia, he obtained a permit to leave the country for these performances and to take his family with him. One cold night just before Christmas in 1917 the Rachmaninoffs crossed the border of Russia to go through Finland to Stockholm. They were never to return to their homeland. Their only possesions were on their backs or in their luggage; everything else they owned, including their beautiful estate at Ivanovka, had been confiscated by the communist authorities.

Rachmaninoff was in debt and had a wife and two little daughters to provide for. He decided that playing the piano was the best way he could provide a livelihood for his family and set about becoming a piano virtuoso. He was 45 years old, his technique was rusty, and his repertory limited, since up to that time his public performances had most often been of his own music. But he immediately began to prepare for a different kind of life and let it be known that he wanted engagements as a piano recitalist. This was the beginning of almost 25 years of the suitcase existence of a solo musician. Enticing offers soon came from the United States, so he crossed the Atlantic a second time, arriving in New York with his family just as the first World War came to an end.

Since they were afraid to return to Russia the family led a rather nomadic existence. Sometimes their home was New York, sometimes Dresden, sometimes a suburb of Paris. As an international concert artist Rachmaninoff usually accepted engagements in the fall and early winter in Europe and on the American continent in the late winter and early spring. Travel by train and ocean liner was time-consuming and exhausting, and there was always the necessity of practicing. He accepted a few invitations to conduct his own orchestral works but again refused to become the conductor of the Boston Symphony Orchestra, and rejected a similar offer from Cincinnati. There was now no time nor energy for composition except during summers, when the concert season was over, and his practice time could be reduced to a minimum. In 1931 the Rachmaninoffs bought property near Lake Lucerne in Switzerland and built a home there. The summers seemed idyllic in these beautiful surroundings, especially when they could have expatriate countrymen join them for all-Russian weekends or week-long parties.

The family finally sold their home in Switzerland and, after a summer in California, bought a new home in Beverly Hills. Because of recurring health problems Rachmaninoff had decided that the season of 1942-1943 would end his concertizing. He was able to carry out only part of a planned tour; his recital in Knoxville, Tennessee, in February of 1943 was the last time he played. The remainder of the tour had to be cancelled, and he returned to California where he died of cancer a few days before his 70th birthday. He had become a citizen of the United States shortly before his death.

Just as there are different evaluations of Rachmaninoff the pianist and Rachmaninoff the composer, there were apparent contradictions between the man and the artist. Rachmaninoff had the reputation of being a cold person—one whose thoughts and feelings were hidden behind a mask. He avoided publicity and interviewers if at all possible. He was slow to speak and notably stingy with words. When he walked on a stage to play a concert—a tall, gaunt, solemn man with rather Mongolian features and the haircut of a convict—his demeanor was indeed austere (Stravinsky once characterized him as a "six-and-a-half-foot-scowl"). For a great deal of his life he was in ill health and suffering from neuralgia. He never felt comfortable expressing himself in English, and with strangers, or when he was in public, he usually felt ill at ease. Friends who saw him at a party when he was feeling well and speaking Russian, found him warm, witty, and bubbling with laughter and high spirits. Similarly, in a recital, after he began to play, one had a very different impression listening to the music he produced. Absolute technical perfection was the rule, but in addition, his tone was sensuously beautiful, his phrasing elegant and free, and his rhythms incisive but flexible. In his playing as in his compositions the man behind the mask was revealed as a sensitive, outgoing person.

THE MUSIC

A story is told about a woman at a cocktail party who asked a rising young pianist about his forthcoming New York recital. When he told her that his program would include a group of Rachmaninoff preludes she replied, "Did you say Rachmaninoff preludes? Oh, did he write more than one?" The story may not be true, but it points up the fact that when many people hear Rachmaninoff's name they think of the famous C-sharp minor prelude, and sometimes they know little more about his music. This piece, written when the composer was just out of the conservatory, brought him early international fame, and it has become one of the most popular piano pieces written in the last hundred years. Its immediate success can be explained in part by the fact that it was sold outright, for a fee worth about $20, to a publisher who didn't get an international copyright. In a short time and ever since, it has appeared in all kinds of editions—some of them titled *The Bells of Moscow*, *The Burning of Moscow*, *The Moscow Waltz*, and even *That Moscow Rag*. For a time the piece was played too frequently—often quite badly—and its composer grew to dislike playing it because it was demanded as an encore at all his piano recitals before the audience would leave the hall. But there are reasons for its popularity other than its ready availability. It is clearly an original, striking, effectively developed musical idea which makes a dramatic impact on the listeners when it is beautifully played.

Rachmaninoff wrote a great deal of other music and probably would have written still more if he had not had careers as conductor and pianist as well as composer. His works include operas, symphonies, symphonic poems, vocal-symphonic music, chamber music, works for piano and orchestra, unaccompanied choral music, music for piano ensemble, over 80 songs, transcriptions of music by other composers, and, needless to say, a great deal of original piano music.

The solo piano music was largely written before 1917 so that most of it has been played and heard for over 65 years without showing signs of reaching retirement age. The most important works in this category began with five pieces published as opus 3 and fashionably entitled *Morceaux de Fantaisie*. The next to follow were the seven pieces in opus 10, entitled *Morceaux de Salon*, and six pieces of opus 16 called *Moments Musicaux*. There are two sonatas, two large sets of variations, two sets of *Etudes-Tableaux* opus 33 and opus 39, and 24 preludes in all the major and minor keys. Unlike the 24 preludes of Chopin, Rachmaninoff's, on the whole, are longer; were published at three different times; and are not arranged in one orderly key sequence. The most famous one, the C-sharp minor prelude, was part of opus 3, published in 1892. The next 10 appeared in 1903 as opus 23, and the remaining 13 were published in 1910 as opus 32. There are a few other pieces of less interest and minor significance, some of which were written as student exercises.

The only work for solo piano which dates from the later part of Rachmaninoff's life is the *Variations on a Theme of Corelli*, op. 42. This work, published in 1931, was played that year for the first time by Rachmaninoff in Montreal. Actually the theme used for variations in this set was not by Corelli but is a melody known as *La Folia* which was common property of a number of 18th century composers. The work is an ingenious set of variations with many of the same characteristics as the dazzling variations on a Paganini theme for piano and orchestra written in 1934, and finally entitled *Rhapsody on a Theme of Paganini*, op. 43.

THIS ANTHOLOGY

This anthology is based on the first editions corrected by the composer and the versions found in *The Complete Works of Rachmaninoff* published in the Soviet Union since 1949. Most of the existing autographs of Rachmaninoff's works are in libraries in Russia, and Soviet librarians are uncooperative about letting foreigners have access to them. The editors of the Russian complete edition who had the use of the manuscripts, however, were very competent and have produced a valuable Urtext, though there are misprints, and the number of copies is severely limited. Obvious errors have been corrected without comment in this edition. Controversial passages are so noted on the pages where they appear.

It is difficult to establish a definitive text for some of Rachmaninoff's music because he, like Chopin, revised in small ways—sometimes several times—what he had written. People who feel that there should be only one correct version of some Rachmaninoff pieces will be disappointed. Consider, for example, the *Sérénade* in B-flat published in 1892 and played by Rachmaninoff and other artists since before the turn of the century. In 1913 Rachmaninoff's cousin and piano teacher, Alexander Siloti, published a "revised version" in which he modified some pianistically awkward passages and changed some dynamic indications, apparently with the composer's approval. For many years this was the version favored by performers. In 1922 Rachmaninoff made a recording of the piece in which he played an embellished version of several passages. Further small changes were introduced in another recording he made in 1936, and a version "revised and as played by the composer," not exactly like any previous one, was published by Charles Foley in 1940. Which of these versions is definitive? One might suppose that the latest version of any given piece was his final and best thought on the matter, but many musicians feel that the curious changes that Rachmaninoff introduced into his early works during the latter part of his life were not improvements on the original. Perhaps they were the result of momentary caprices, or were invented as a relief from the possible boredom of always performing a piece in exactly the same way. The *Humoresque* and the *Barcarolle* are other examples of works the composer changed with variant versions of certain passages. If a definitive version of some of the pieces is impossible to attain, it may also be unnecessary. Perhaps we should be satisfied with one version from the composer, remembering that quibbling over insignificant details is fruitless, and that the spirit is more important than the letter. This edition uses the earliest version of all the pieces except for the *Sérénade* which, for reasons of practicality, adopts details from two of the later versions.

Rachmaninoff seldom wrote metronome marks for his piano music except for the preludes of opus 23. Both before and after that publication of 1903 he apparently thought it better not to be as specific as possible about tempos. Most musicians agree that the precise tempo for a performance should be governed to a degree by the instrument, the resonance of the room, and the taste and skill of the player.

Rachmaninoff probably would have accepted modifications of his metronome marks. All the pieces in this collection bear the composer's tempo marks in cases where they exist. For those pieces that have no metronome marks from the composer the suggested metronome marks are indicated thus: (♩ = c. 80). The fingering given here is largely new. Rachmaninoff wrote fairly complete fingerings for a few of his pieces (though not for any in this collection), but for the most part he wrote fingering only for unusual or particularly complex passages. Some of his fingering is excellent for anyone and has been retained here, but since he was a tall man with king-size hands some of his fingerings are impractical for small or average-size hands. There will never be agreement about the best fingering for many passages because such judgments are based on the size and flexibility of the hands, on previous training, and on the old habits of different individuals. The fingerings offered here are serviceable for the average size hand, and some facilitations incorporated in this edition will ease some of the playing difficulties. No apology is offered for these; if one can play all the notes the composer wrote in an easier rather than a harder way and achieve equally good musical results, the learning process will be shorter and the performance more secure. Concert artists take advantage of such helps; why should students not do so as well? Fingerings from any source should be regarded as suggestions for a convenient, efficient way of reaching the best musical results.

The use of the arms in playing this music is a matter of utmost importance, but unfortunately it can't be indicated in the music in any practical, comprehensible way.

The use of the damper pedal for this music is also a matter of greatest importance, though Rachmaninoff seldom indicated pedaling. He wrote it for unusual passages, and completely for only one piece, leaving the large part of his piano music without pedal indications. Good pedaling has to be coordinated with fingering, and is dependent on the resonance of the piano, the reflected sound from the room, the tempos, the dynamic levels and balances involved, and the skill of the performer. Though the modern way of indicating pedaling is an improvement over the older pedal indications (Ped. *), it is not completely satisfactory, since some of the most beautiful and subtle pedaling results from depressing the pedal to different depths. Particularly important is the technique of depressing the pedal barely enough to lift the dampers off the strings so that changes can be accomplished with maximum speed. The kind of half pedaling which briefly seats the dampers so lightly on the strings that the upper strings are damped while the lower strings continue to sound is also of great value. These refined pedal effects are impossible to notate in the music. They must be arrived at by experiment and careful listening during practice. The pedaling given here should serve the student during the learning process and should be a point of departure for later, more subtle use of the damper pedal.

GENERAL SUGGESTIONS

Trills in Rachmaninoff's music start on the given note, not on the upper auxiliary as in the music of the 18th century. Rolled chords are frequent and should be done with minimum disruption of the rhythmic pulse. With few exceptions broadening the tempo as the music moves toward the rolled chord is desirable, so that the lowest notes of the chord start slightly early, and the top note arrives on the delayed beat. If the rolled chord starts in the bass the pedal should go down on the lowest note before the finger leaves the key, so that the lowest note—the harmonic bass for the rest of the chord—continues to sound. People with large hands can often play large rolled chords by relaxing the wrist and each finger after it has played its key, while swinging the elbow to the right, usually with a high wrist. People with average or small hands must experiment to find the best way for them to roll these widely spaced chords. Some will find it easiest to start a right hand four-or five-note rolled chord spanning a tenth with the second finger, the thumb and other fingers following upward in the obvious order. This is particularly true if the tempo is not fast. Other people will find it easier to start such a chord with the thumb and put the third or fourth finger over the fifth at the top of the chord. This is particularly useful if the top note is a black key which follows a white. However they are played, these chords should sound graceful rather than strained, should fit the dynamic context, and should be evenly balanced dynamically with all the sounds equidistant in time. These and other works can best be studied, memorized, and performed if the form of the music is clear in the player's mind. In other words, if the student sees how the composer has put the piece together he or she is better able to practice it intelligently (using sections and subsections for practice segments), memorize it efficiently, and concentrate on it during the performance. The interpretation of the music will be more convincing if matters of form are understood, since interpreting music is concerned with clarifying for the listener similarities and differences in the music. Rachmaninoff's early works usually have clear-cut sections and subsections, but in the later works these points of arrival and departure are often disguised by subtle craftsmanship which makes the piece flow connectedly from beginning to end but which obscures the articulations for the learner. The brief analyses which follow, together with practice suggestions, should help persons unfamiliar with these pieces to begin their study effectively.

THE PIECES

PRELUDE IN C-SHARP MINOR, Op. 3, No. 2—page 11

Rachmaninoff denied that he had any descriptive idea in mind when he wrote this prelude, though it is not surprising that people have thought so, because the music immediately establishes a mood of great seriousness. Sustaining the whole and half notes on the first page is a problem best solved by the use of the sostenuto pedal, but since many pianos do not have this expensive device, the first page is printed here with an alternate version in which the left hand little finger can quickly take one of the low notes played by the right hand, to hold it while half pedaling retains part of the sound of the lowest bass notes.

The tempo set by the three opening notes should be held steady up to measure 14. The middle section is faster as indicated, and the up-stemmed melody notes should stand out against the bass line while the second and third notes of the triplet are softer. The right hand part can be practiced by blocking the chords—playing all the notes on one beat at the same time (except for those places as in measure 17 where there is an up-stemmed eighth note, which can be played after the chord)—as far as the middle of measure 35. At the end of measures 27, 28, 30, and 31 it is necessary to broaden the beats so that the long jump for the left hand won't give the rhythm a disturbing wrench. The cadenza of interlocked chords which begins in measure 35 can also be practiced by playing simultaneously all the notes on one beat. By this means the sound of the chords and the feel of the keyboard positions are clearly established in the student's mind before the accents alternating between the hands introduce a further complication. Measures 43 and 44 establish by augmentation the opening motif and should re-establish the original tempo.

From measure 45, when four staves are used simultaneously, maximum sonority can be achieved only by using maximum weight of the arm. Again at the end of measure 50 and measure 52 the tempo must be broadened so that the continuity of the pulse is bent but not broken, as both hands move from the low to the high chords written on the first beat. The coda, which begins at measure 55, may be done with a diminuendo; since all the chords have C-sharps in addition to the low C-sharps (the pedal-point in the bass), the new elements in each chord may be stressed lightly.

POLICHINELLE, Op. 3, No. 4—Page 17

The name of this piece means *Punch*, a character in the Punch and Judy puppet shows popular years ago in many parts of Europe. Traditionally, Punch was an ugly puppet with a hump back and hook nose and chin, who boasted a great deal and beat his nagging wife. As the music begins one can imagine him jumping onto the stage, moving with a shuffle to disappear on the opposite side, and then repeating the action from the opposite direction. After the introduction (as the play begins) it is easy to hear in the music his alternate loud boasting, sly threats, and terrible rages.

The form of this piece is clearly ternary. Bringing out the melody in the middle section, which begins at measure 59, is not difficult since the melody is doubled in the lower octave, but the student should be concerned in this section with shaping each of the four-measure phrases to emphasize the longer notes. The return of the first section, abbreviated but amplified with thicker chords, is the most difficult part of the piece, particularly for those with small hands.

SÉRÉNADE, Op. 3, No. 5—Page 27

This piece summons up an atmosphere of Spain and a love song being sung with guitar accompaniment. It starts with a feeling of delightful uncertainty because a root position tonic chord does not occur until measure 59. The introduction has the quality of an improvisation before the song proper begins at measure 31. An interlude with seductive chromatic harmony begins at measure 62. At measure 74 the song is continued with interruptions from the interlude, and the piece moves forward with song and interlude alternating. The song has been in the range of a tenor voice until measure 110, but there it goes into a higher octave. Does this mean that the lady, after a hesitant beginning, replies with her version of the song? What is the meaning of the coda, with 17 measures of delicate interlude and a very loud final measure? A simple surprise, or a triumph?

BARCAROLLE, Op. 10, No. 3—Page 32

This piece in the tradition of Mendelssohn, Chopin, and others is music inspired by the boat songs of Venetian gondoliers. The accompaniment pattern which starts the piece suggests water gently lapping against the side of a boat. The song-like melody with its hesitant rhythm is in the range of a man's voice. It is easiest to think of this rhythm in pairs of measures, as though it were written in 6/4 rather than in 3/4 meter, but the main difficulty lies in keeping both melody and accompaniment light, buoyant, and graceful. In the middle of this ternary form the triplets and quarter notes are exchanged for more flowing 16th notes (measure 71), and the tonality wavers between G minor and B-flat. At the end of this section (measure 111), as the 16th notes break into a cadenza, the student may find the learning process facilitated by mentally shifting the bar lines to think of the passage as if it were in 2/4 time. The third large section, where the original melody is combined with the 16th note motion of the middle section (measure 125), multiplies the complexities, making this the most difficult section of the piece. The long coda which begins at measure 173 brings the work to a graceful close.

MÉLODIE, Op. 10, No. 4—Page 44

The main problem in playing this piece is one of balance—keeping the melody in the foreground and shaped into well-rounded phrases, while the rolled chords of the accompaniment keep their place as background. The difficulty is especially acute when a melody note occurs in the middle of a chord with accompanying notes both above and below it. The middle section of this ternary form is in strong contrast to the opening, since it changes the meter, the tempo, and the tonality. The return of the *Allegretto* in 3/8 at measure 98 is enriched with contrapuntal imitations which should be made clear. The return of the *Allegro moderato* material brings that part of the piece into the main tonal center of E, though it is E major rather than E minor.

HUMORESQUE, Op. 10, No. 5—Page 50

The meaning of this title is contained in its first two syllables. Since humor often depends on surprises, the piece is full of unexpected contrasts of dynamics. It begins with a whimsical 18-measure introduction which also serves as a coda and as a means of articulating the three large sections of the piece. At measure 59 and similar places, the melody is in the upper notes of the left hand and the lower notes of the right hand—usually played by the two thumbs—and is usefully practiced without the chords. So far as evenness in time is concerned, it is helpful to practice the left hand alone, making sure that all the chords are equidistant in time and adding the right hand part later. The middle section, which begins at measure 84, introduces a wistful mood in contrast to the first and last parts. Measure 176 seems to be something new, but it is a variant on the idea first presented in measure 59. The most difficult problem in this work is that of making the melody stand out from the thickly written harmony. The carefully marked dynamic contrasts are of greatest importance in playing the piece well.

MOMENT MUSICAL, Op. 16, No. 5—Page 59

This next-to-the-last of the "musical moments," op. 16, is the most lyrical of the set. A quiet melody like a lullaby emerges over a gently rocking bass figure which moves away from D-flat as its lowest note for only three measures of the piece. At the beginning, two two-measure phrases are followed by one of three, and another of two. The next nine measures are a varied version of the original nine. The middle section, which starts at measure 20, is made up of six-beat phrases until measure 28 when the phrases begin to assume various lengths, and the tension of the dissonances is intensified until the lowest bass note moves a minor third in effect for the three measures preceding the return. The last section of the piece, starting at measure 38, combines phrases from both the original and the varied version of the opening nine measures, with embellishing interpolations in a different dynamic which suggest a contrast of orchestral color. Most difficult are measures 43 and 45, when the right hand has to control the two elements simultaneously. The last seven measures are a coda.

PRELUDE IN D, Op. 23, No. 4—Page 64

This prelude in this edition has a different distribution of the notes between the hands from that found in other editions, though comparison with the original edition or with any of the reprints will show that no notes have been omitted or changed. Players who have a sostenuto pedal on their pianos may experiment by putting down the key for the first note of the piece—the low D—silently, setting the sostenuto on it before starting to play, and then pedaling as usual. This will give added resonance to the first 10 measures which all develop from the tonic chord. (The sostenuto must be released, of course, at the beginning of measure 11.) For those with average size hands the first right hand chord at measure 16, and one like it later in the piece, can be played by bending the thumb outward at the nail knuckle over the C-sharp and the D, or by quickly sliding the thumb from the black to the white key.

After two measures of a quiet accompaniment figure on the tonic chord, a close-knit lyric melody unfolds for 16 measures. The next 16 measures, in spite of harmonic changes, are essentially a variation on the first 16, with the melody in a middle register and a counterpoint above it over rolled chords. The next section of the piece, starting at measure 35, begins with the original melody in diminution expanding and developing the resulting motif against flowing triplets in the bass until it achieves a powerful climax at measure 51. Measure 53 begins the last section, another variation on the original melody, now heard in the upper register with a countertheme above it. A five-measure coda is reminiscent of the third section.

PRELUDE IN G MINOR, Op. 23, No. 5—Page 69

This second-most-popular Rachmaninoff piano piece was written before the others in the opus but published as part of the book of 10 preludes. The first and last parts of this ternary form are buoyant, military march music and are themselves small ternary forms. Eight measures—17 to 24—make up a brief middle section, with the similar passage in the last part serving the same function. Because the over-all effect is vigorous and aggressive, and because the hands must make long jumps quickly, one is tempted to play it all loudly, but the dynamic markings will show that this was not the composer's intention.

The lyrical center section is richly resonant, and the first two two-measure phrases are played lightly with long pedals as the left arm moves the hand quickly and close to the keys from one placement to another. At measures 39 and 40 the line of the real bass moves downward as the volume of sound increases. The difficult part of this section begins at the end of measure 41, when a countermelody in the middle register moves from left hand to right and back again. This can best be accomplished by using arm weight or pressure from the upper arm which must be equalized between left and right hands. The addition of the countermelody produces more tension and more interest; when well played the effect is rich and powerful. The end of the piece is a gradual tapering off as though the marchers were disappearing in the distance, and the last three measures are surprisingly evanescent.

PRELUDE IN E-FLAT, Op. 23, No. 6—Page 77

The difficult problems of playing this attractive piece are those of subtle pedaling, of playing the left hand 16th notes lightly while making the main harmonic changes clear, and of giving adequate bass support to the right hand chords. If one thinks of the first measure as an upbeat, the first phrase, ending at measure 5, is balanced by a second, ending at measure 9, which tips the tonality toward G minor. The following five measures extend and develop the melodic idea, taking the tonality through F minor back to E-flat. Measure 14 begins a longer flight of developed melody which moves by way of the subdominant and the supertonic to cadence, dominant to tonic, at measure 23. The thick texture of filled-in octaves now disappears as the opening theme, simplified and extended in a new way, begins in a lower register as a single, undoubled line. The filled-in octaves are resumed briefly to enrich a high, soft climax. Measure 31 begins two-part writing for the right hand—a kind of dialogue for soprano and alto. The coda, starting at measure 39, derives from the left hand accompanying figure with which the piece began.

PRELUDE IN G-FLAT, Op. 23, No. 10—Page 82

This prelude is technically rather easy for about three-fourths of the total length but has some knotty difficulties in about 10 measures, and the interpretative problems are not easy to solve. The pulsing accompaniment which surges up from dominant to tonic in its lower voice as the piece begins sets the mood and tempo, as well as presenting a motif to be used later. A tranquil, nostalgic melody begins in the left hand with a falling fifth from dominant to tonic and develops two four-measure phrases. The last beat of measure 10 begins a duet-like passage in which the treble voice freely imitates the lower voice. Measure 18 starts a rising sequence of melodic fragments and chords with a quickening rhythmic pattern and a crescendo which leads to a climax of great power before it diminishes to a long D-flat at measure 33.

This note is the beginning of the baritone melody (D-flat to G-flat) heard at the beginning of the piece, though the fact is obscured by the length of the first note, and by the two notes which fill in part of the interval with two downward steps toward the G-flat in measure 35. The left hand now continues this melody with the figure from the accompaniment of the first measure, as the right hand plays a high countermelody and light, syncopated chords. The second phrase of this complex texture is extended until it slows and stops completely on a supertonic chord; it moves to another supertonic in measure 46, to be followed in the same measure by a dominant seventh which leads to the tonic pedal point extending through most of the coda. Measure 47 presents again the accompanying figure from the first measure, and the high G-flat in measure 48 begins the falling interval of the opening baritone melody with the tones reversed. The gently rolling triplets in the bass, a new rhythmic element, and the wide-spread rolled chords create a sumptuous sound as elements of the tonal structure are piled together vertically and horizontally for a lavish soft climax. The falling-fourth sequential patterns move over a tonic pedal point until the texture thins, and the falling intervals now rise in sequence from the bass toward a sustained tonic chord and a concluding strong cadence.

PRELUDE IN B-FLAT MINOR, Op. 32, No. 2—Page 84

This prelude is original and unique in several respects. First, it is dominated by a rhythmic motif—a dotted 8th followed by a 16th and an 8th (♪. ♬)—which is the upbeat to the first measure and which, incidentally, occurs frequently in several other preludes in this opus. Second, it is tonally ambiguous, avoiding a tonic chord until the very end of the piece, somewhat like a narrative whose significance becomes apparent only in the last paragraph. Third, it has a variety of tempos and moods; and fourth, it has irregular phrase lengths which are obscured by the placement of the bar lines. The student must be aware of the length of the phrases growing out of the repeated, developing motif in order to keep the piece moving forward by phrases rather than letting it break into fragments. Not counting the upbeat, the first phrase lasts through the first two measures (seven beats); the second is eight beats long; the next, four; the next, three; and the next, nine.

The harmonic structure is centered around ornamented chords of the dominant and the dominant of the dominant, perhaps giving the impression that F is the tonal center. The balancing eight measures of this subsection begin at the *tempo primo* of measure 9, presenting a varied version of the opening. The second large section of this ternary form starts delicately at measure 17, moves through a series of more and more exciting sequential patterns to a high, powerful, scintillating climax around the dominant before it grows calmer and spirals down to a low F, the bass of the dominant seventh chord, at measure 35. The two-measure transition marked *Meno mosso* sounds the opening motif in augmentation, while B-flats are heard for the first time in the bass, hinting at the real tonality. The *Allegro moderato* marks the beginning of five beats more of transition over the dominant, which lead to a return of the opening on the second beat of measure 38, but now the phrases are all eight beats long. The *Allegro scherzando* creates a light, playful atmosphere. Two measures later the texture thins, and the bass moves from three long dominants (the low F's in measures 49, 50, and 51) to the tonic of B-flat as the lowest bass note. Was this whole piece an elaborate bit of magic, keeping the true goal of the motion out of the listener's hearing until the last two measures?

PRELUDE IN G, Op. 32, No. 5—Page 90

This serenely beautiful, contemplative piece exploits the upper register of the piano, and requires carefully judged balances and a beautiful tone. After the murmuring accompaniment has set the rhythm in motion, an elegant, meditative melody is introduced in the upper register, to be interrupted at the end of measure 6 by a rippling 32nd note figure followed by a peaceful comment in the bass. A varied version of the first part begins at the end of measure 10, but this time the 32nd note figure leads into a middle section which develops this figure over a six-measure dominant, ending in trills and a six-measure change to the minor mode. The principal theme returns again at measure 28 in a still different version, and this leads into a diaphanous coda, starting at the second beat of measure 35, which is derived from the first few notes of the opening melody in diminution. The complexly related rhythms are one major hurdle to learning this piece, because they should be precise as well as easy and flowing. The lyric melody should always have a warm, singing sound and should be shaped toward the high climactic notes.

PRELUDE IN F, Op. 32, No. 7—Page 95

Unlike the second prelude of opus 32, this prelude makes its tonality clear at once. The tonic triad is sounded in the first measure, and many half-step moves away from and back to the triad in all of the voices ensue, before a move to the dominant in measure 5 and one back to the tonic in measure 7. Though this edition gives a different distribution of notes between the hands from the original, making some of the playing easier, this prelude is best for a player with large hands since the keyboard reaches are very wide. Players who have a sostenuto pedal may want to experiment with its use in this prelude by silently pressing the key for the F two octaves below middle C and setting the sostenuto on it before the playing begins. It may be a surprise to hear how the resonance is changed, and to hear how long it is possible to keep this added aura before the release of the sostenuto becomes necessary.

At the beginning of the piece the lower line is melodic, as is the upper line with its longer note values, while the bouncing inner voice must be in a softer dynamic level. At measure 13 the harmony passes through a supertonic to reach a dominant in measures 15 and 16 before the opening phrase is heard a second time. At the *Piu vivo* the bass begins to crawl upward and the upper line starts to move more quickly; the texture thickens, the dissonances and the harmony, further from the tonal center, produce more tension, and a crescendo builds toward a resonant climax at measure 27. But there is soon a return to the original four-voice texture as well as to the original bass line. In the first of the four-measure phrases that begin at measure 34, the upper line swings ecstatically from C, the dominant, to the C an octave higher, to F, the tonic, and returns to a long C and a flourish away from and back to that C, while a chromatic melody in the middle register, interwoven with flowing 16th notes, slithers up and down over a bass line which strongly supports the F major tonality. The second of these phrases reverses the structural notes for the upper line, going from F to F, to C, and back to F. The four measure coda, after a small surprise, brings us back to the original melodic and harmonic ideas and an ethereal ending.

PRELUDE IN B MINOR, Op. 32, No. 10—Page 99

This prelude—another which uses the rhythmic motif of a dotted 8th, a 16th, and an 8th—was a favorite of Rachmaninoff. It was inspired by a painting called *The Return* by the Swiss artist Arnold Böcklin, which shows a man in the dress of another age, his image reflected in a pool, sitting with his back to the viewer and gazing down into a dark valley where there is a house with a lighted window. Is the house his home? Why is he pausing here? Is he returning alone rather than with someone else? The picture is enigmatic, and to some extent the prelude is as well. The tempo and rhythm suggest someone walking with faltering footsteps. This prelude has somber, dark-hued harmonies and a grandeur not found in some of the other preludes.

The form is clearly ternary with a rather regular phrase structure. The opening four-measure phrase is followed by one that is extended by two measures, before the ascending and descending sequential figures begin at measure 10. The second large section of the piece starts at measure 18. It must be played with arm weight to give it very powerful resonance, but care must be taken that the repeated chords do not become too heavy for the long notes of the melody in the middle register. A long transition begins at *L'istesso tempo;* more and more excited rhythms accrue over an F-sharp (dominant) pedal point until the meter changes to 3/4 and the subdominant seventh chord, with E as its bass, prevails, finally breaking into a cadenza. The final section, which starts at the end of measure 48, is a much abbreviated return to the first part. The piece concludes with a sighing two-measure coda.

PRELUDE IN B, Op. 32, No. 11—Page 104

This prelude makes rather few technical demands on the player. It too uses the rhythm of the dotted 8th, a 16th, and an 8th, but this time the melodies, influenced by Russian Orthodox chants, are harmonized with many root position triads, producing a simple, archaic effect. The two major difficulties in playing this piece are those of achieving long lines from a mosaic-like assemblage of short fragments—the melodic motifs which are the structural elements—and of avoiding confusion when playing the piece from memory. The closely related melodic motifs undergo rhythmic and harmonic transformations, or reappear in a different order, so that careful analysis, and concentration while performing are necessary for the student to avoid the pitfalls.

The piece begins with a four-measure phrase which is then repeated without its upbeat, these eight measures being balanced by two two-measure phrases and another of four measures which comes to rest suspensefully on an augmented triad. The succeeding pair of two-measure phrases is followed by nine measures which contain a harmonic surprise, and then the piece apparently starts over from the beginning, but only for four measures. Though measure 34 is like measure 13, the continuation is different. Changes of meter which begin at measure 50 introduce faint bell-like sounds in the upper register, and bring about some elongated repetitions of what has already been heard. Compare measures 54 and 55 with measures 19 and 20; likewise compare 57 and 58 with 17 and 18, and 59 and 60 with 36 and 37. A three-measure phrase which begins at measure 73 ends the main body of the piece, and a long coda with contrasted registers, beginning at measure 76, uses two- and three-measure phrases to bring the work to a close.

ETUDE-TABLEAU IN G MINOR, Op., 33, No. 8—Page 108

The title of this piece means *pictorial study*. The picture the composer had in mind was never revealed, but like a study by Chopin, Debussy, or some other composer, it presents playing problems to be solved by the performer. In this case the problems are those of making the melodies sing, achieving contrasted dynamics and sonorities, and finding a convincing interpretation. Though not obviously so, the piece is monothematic.

After a measure setting the key, it begins in a rather conventional way with a four-measure phrase which starts with repeated B-flats. The latter half of measure 4 and measure 5 contain a descending-scale bass figure which seems to be a simple reply to the opening melodic statement. Actually it is a restatement of the opening phrase in diminution, with a long note substituted for the repeated B-flats. Like a detail in a narrative which is introduced casually but becomes increasingly important, this melodic fragment soon dominates the piece. After another four-measure phrase (beginning at measure 6) which is developed from the original statement, the reply appears in the treble enriched with second inversion chords. From here it moves to the bass, to a middle register, to the treble again, and back to the bass, where it quickens and leads to a dramatic recitative-like outburst (measures 16, 17, and 18). From measure 19, the parallel second-inversion chords are developed by sequence and inversion until a cadenza over the dominant occurs, its descending lower line derived from the original theme, which has appeared in many guises. A surprising chord and a flourish introduce another recitative-like passage, which leads to a modified return. (Compare measure 36 and what follows with the passage that begins at measure 10.) At measure 41 the quickened rhythmic pattern found in the bass in measure 15, starts in the treble and, by a two-octave downward sequence, speeds to powerful low G's two octaves apart, and a brilliant rising scale. Two soft tonic chords conclude the piece.

(Please turn to page 113.)

PRELUDE in C-sharp Minor

(the first 13 measures for pianos without a sostenuto pedal) (Half-pedal carefully)

Op. 3, No. 2
(1892)

Although it has often been printed, recorded, and misread as D natural, the D-sharp in the left hand, here and in measure 48, is correct.

PRELUDE in C-sharp Minor

For pianos with a sostenuto pedal

Ⓢ = depress sostenuto after keys are down

* = release sostenuto

Op. 3, No. 2
(1892)

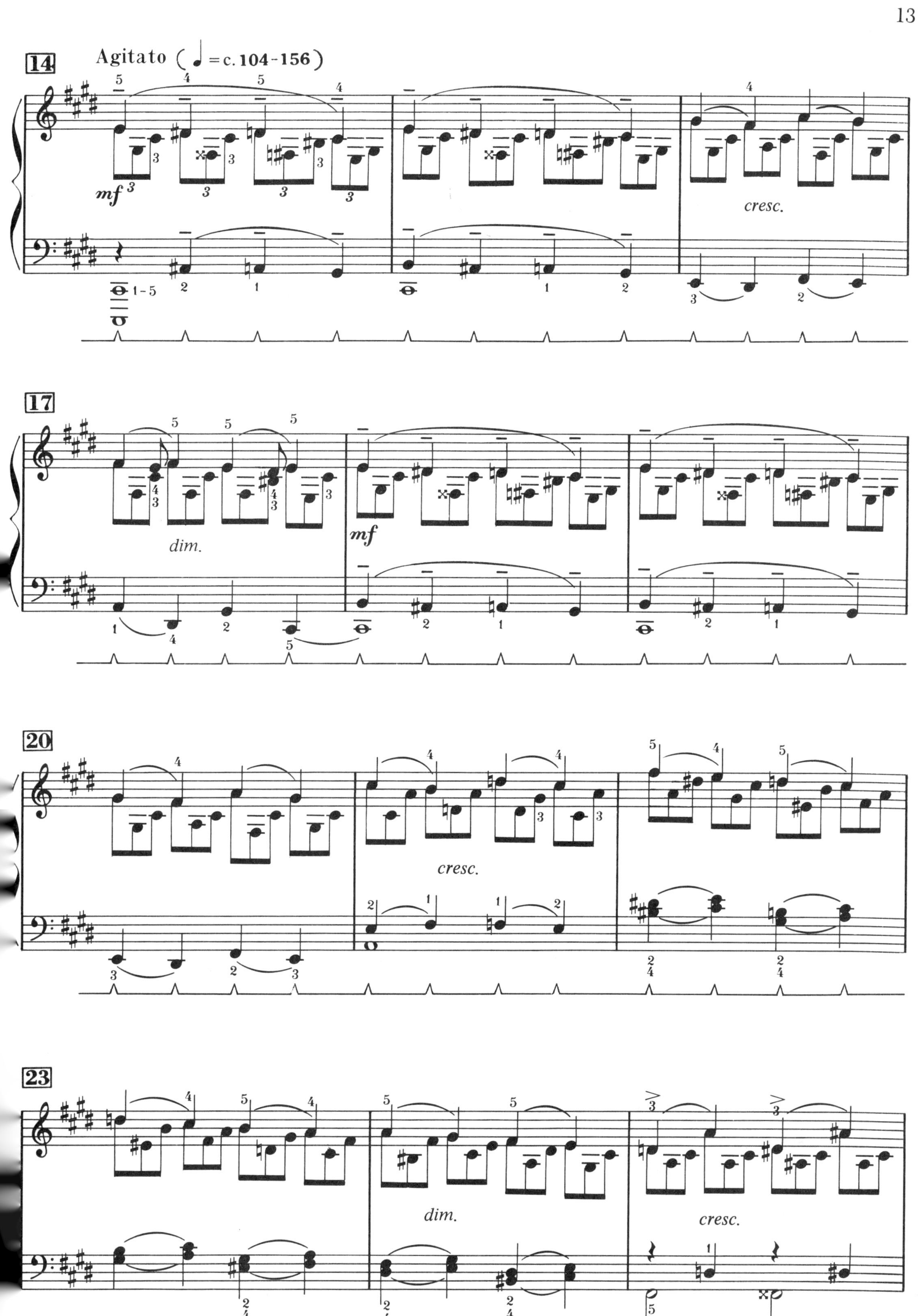
14
Agitato (♩ = c. 104-156)
mf
cresc.
17
dim.
mf
20
cresc.
23
dim.
cresc.

26
ff
half ped.
Ped. sim.
29
dim.
32
cresc.
35
accel.
fff

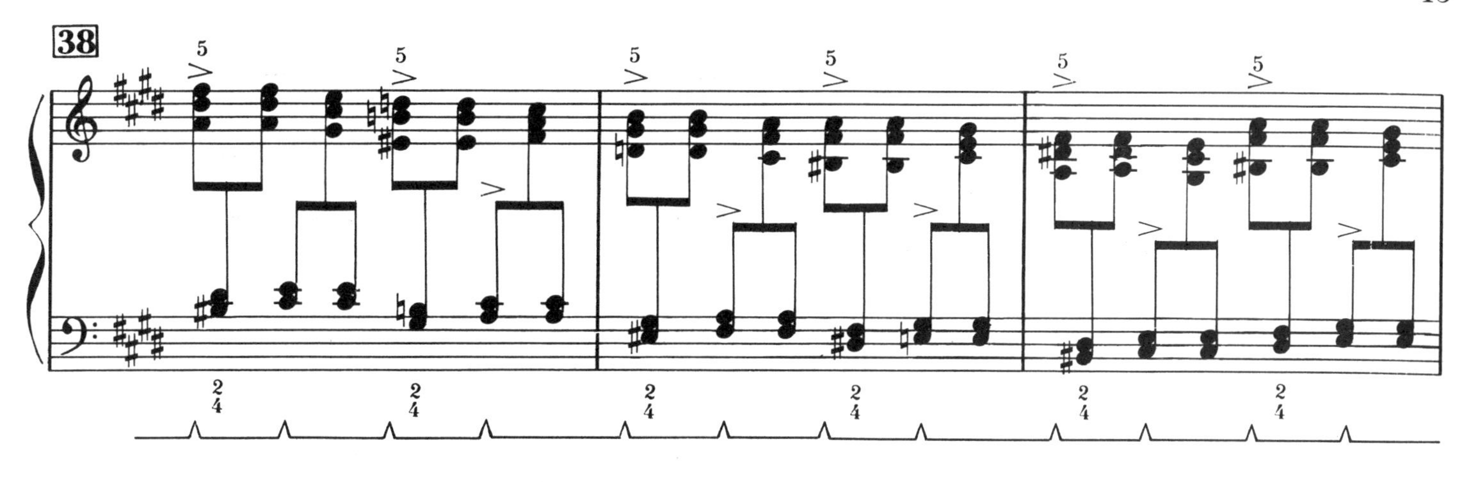
38

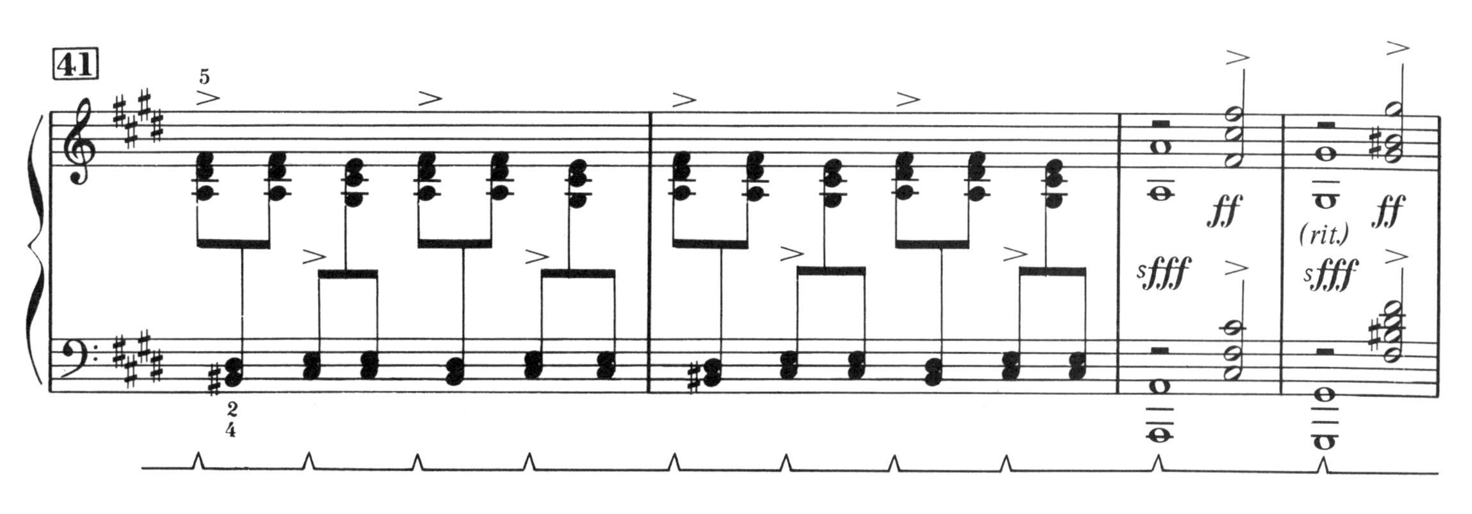
41
ff
sfff
(rit.)
ff
sfff

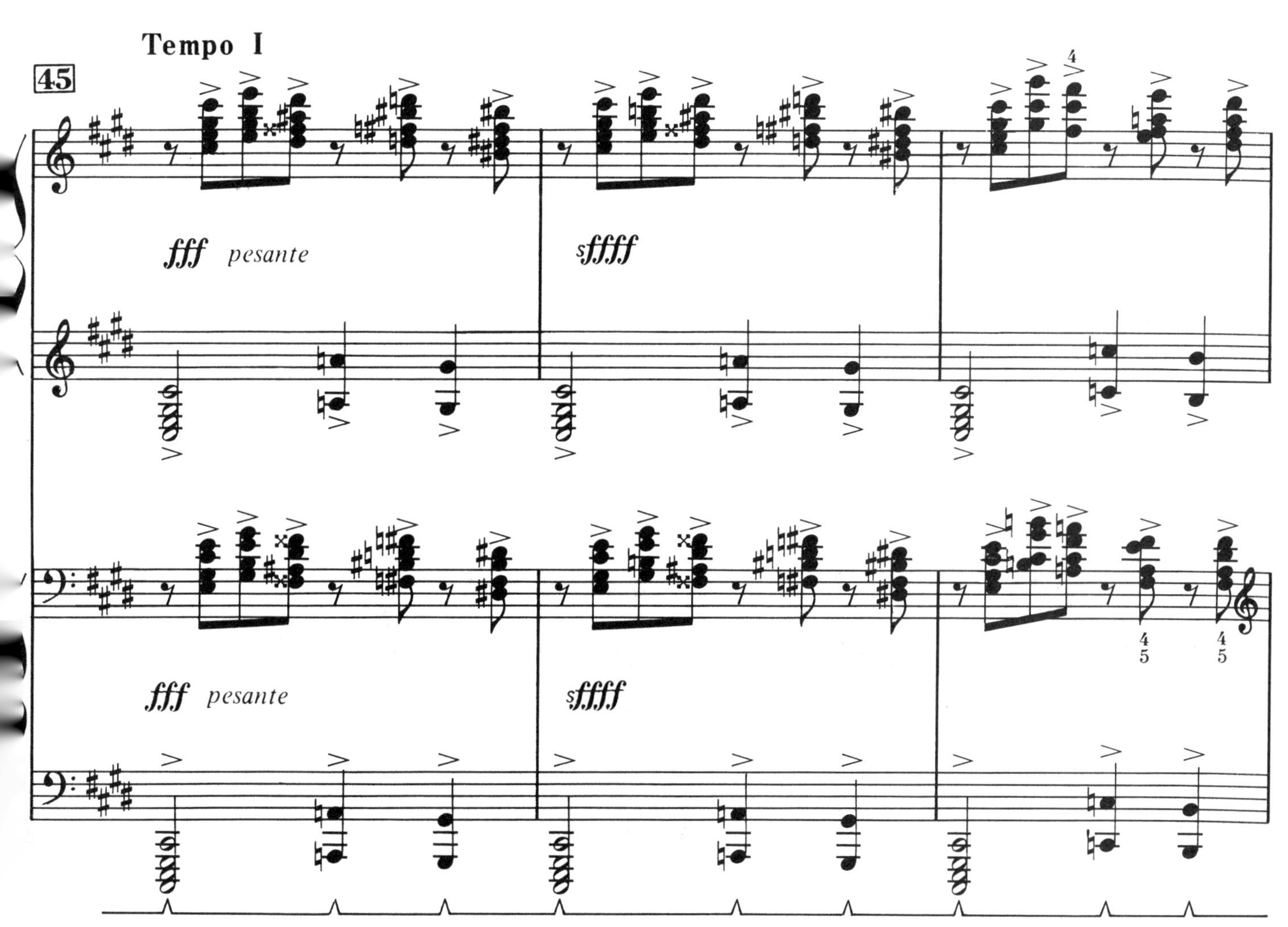
Tempo I
45
fff pesante
sffff
fff pesante
sffff

48
sffff
sffff
51
dim.
dim.
54
dim.
dim.
mf
mf
ppp
ppp

POLICHINELLE in F-sharp Minor

Op. 3, No. 4
(1892)

** The *forte* indications in parentheses in measures 3, 7, 94, and 98 do not appear in the Russian editions.

17
ff
21
p
ff
25
p
ff
28
8va
sfff

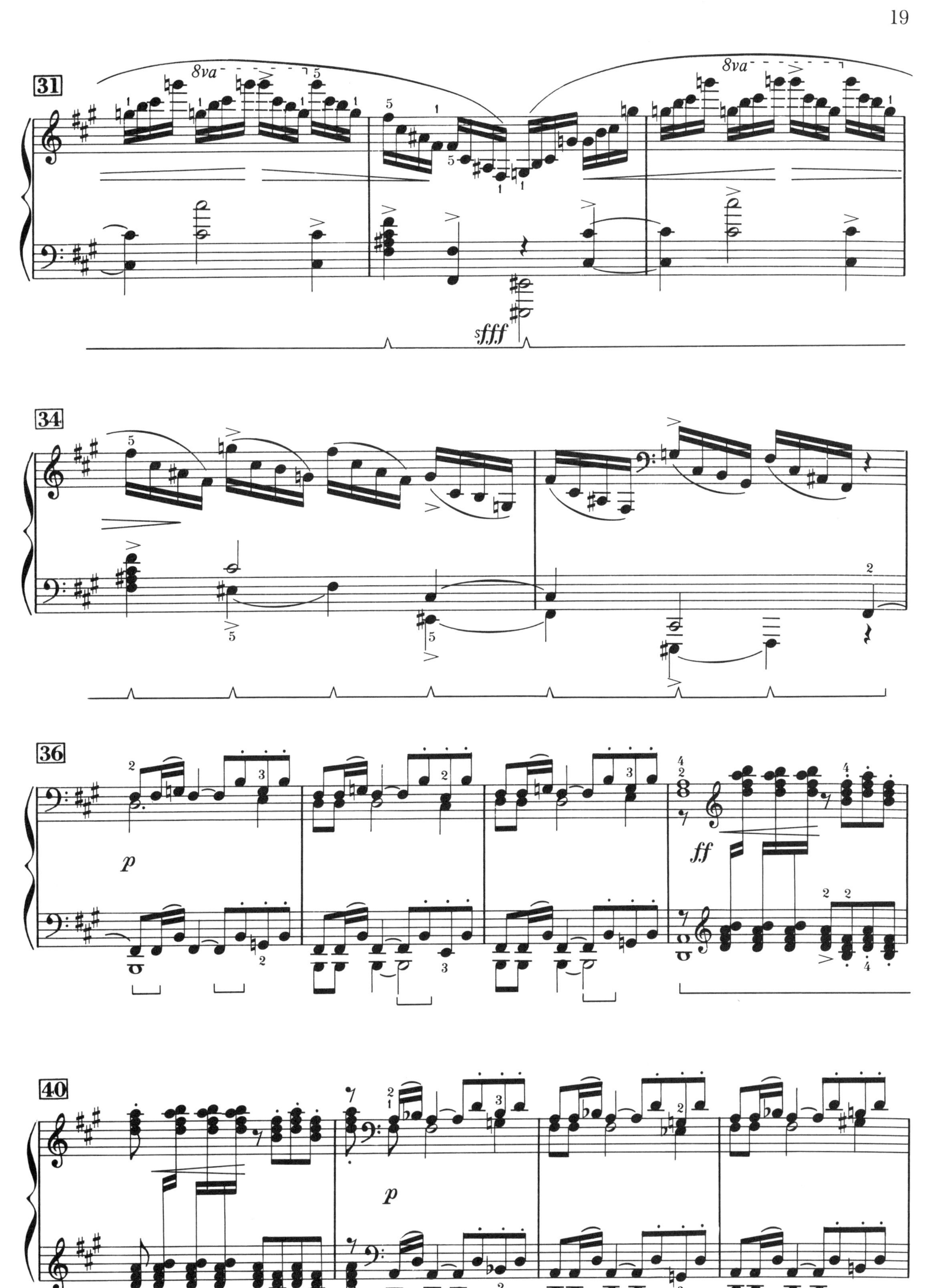

31
8va
sfff
34
36
p
ff
40
p

44
ff
p
47
8va
ff
50
8va
sfff
sfff
53
8va

55
59
Agitato
f
62
65
dim.
p

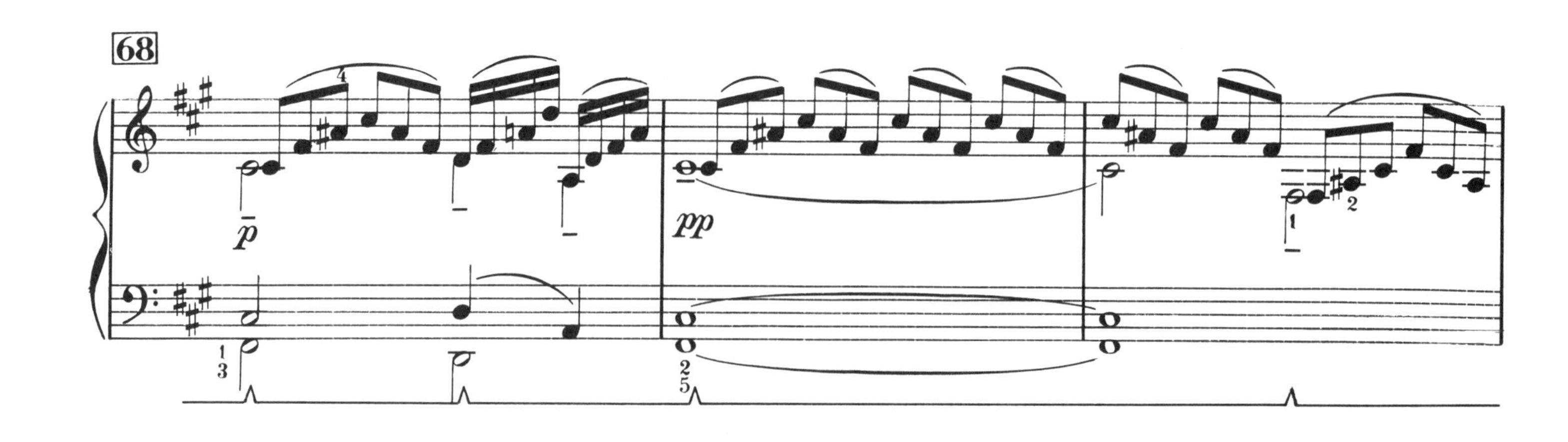
68
p
pp

71
f

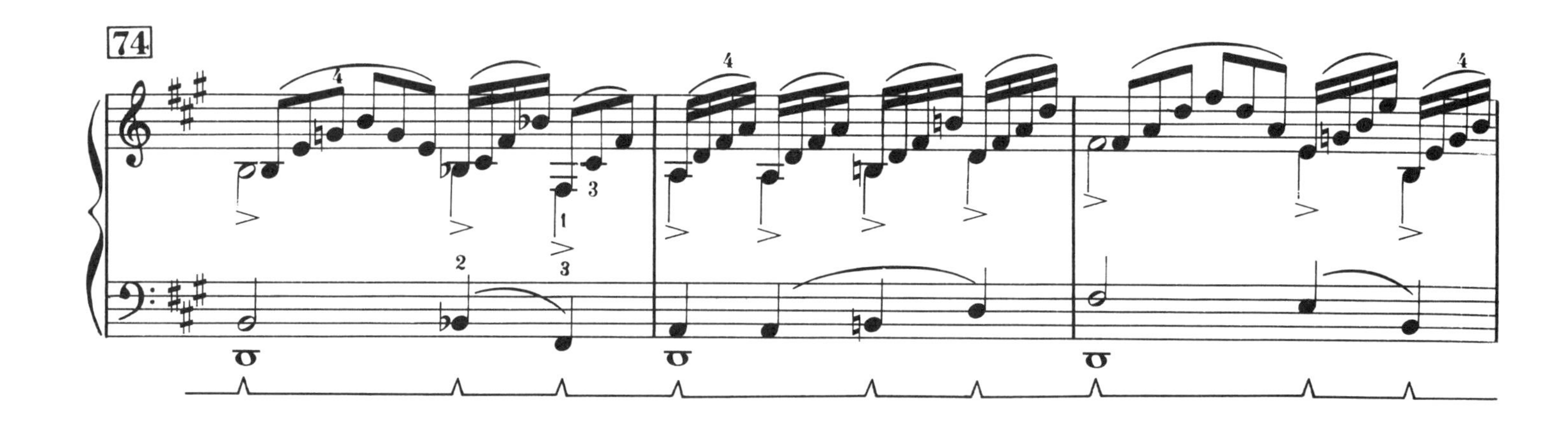
74

77
dim.
p

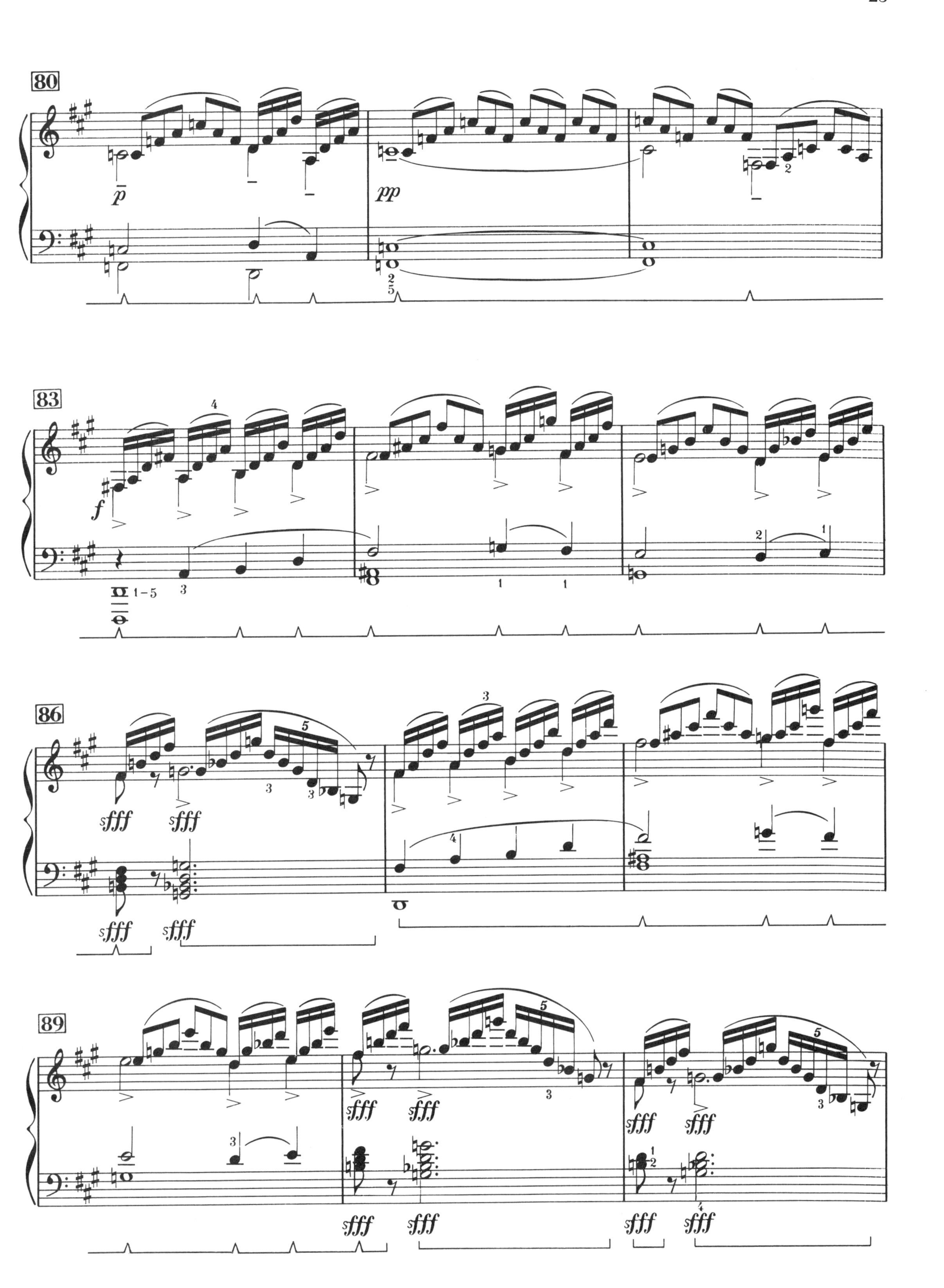
80
p
pp
83
f
86
sfff
89

92
sfff
ppp
(f)
96
p
(f)
101
ff
105
f

109
fff
112
f
115
8va
fff
f
118
ff
8va

121
8va
5
1
1
sfff
123
8va
1
sfff
125
8va
5
127
8va
1
3
1
3
fff
1
3
3
8va
4
5
3
1
3
1
4
5

SÉRÉNADE in B-flat Minor

* In a recording Rachmaninoff played several passages of this piece with embellishments.

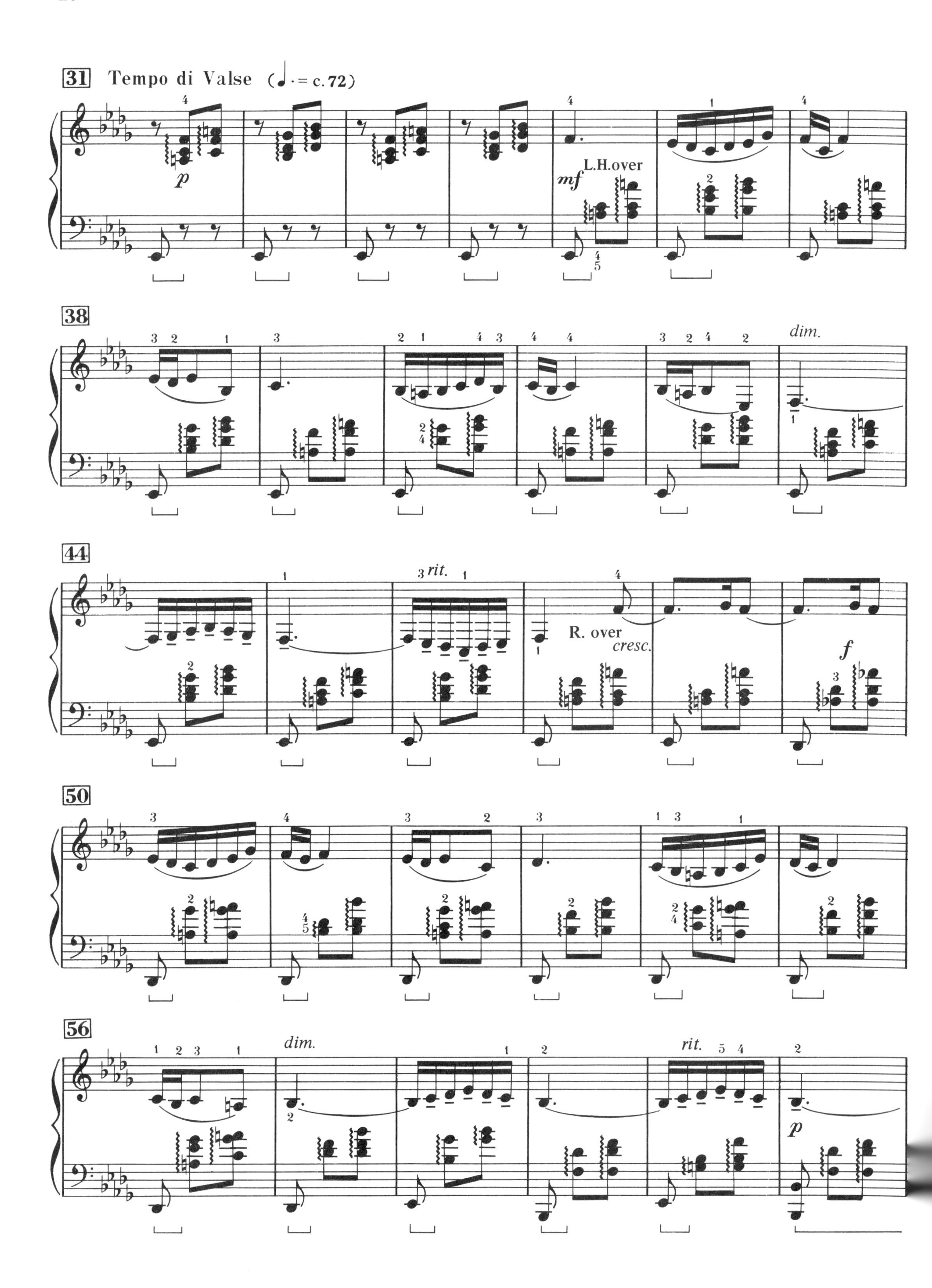
31
Tempo di Valse
(♩. = c. 72)
p
mf
L.H.over
38
dim.
44
rit.
R. over
cresc.
f
50
56
dim.
rit.
p

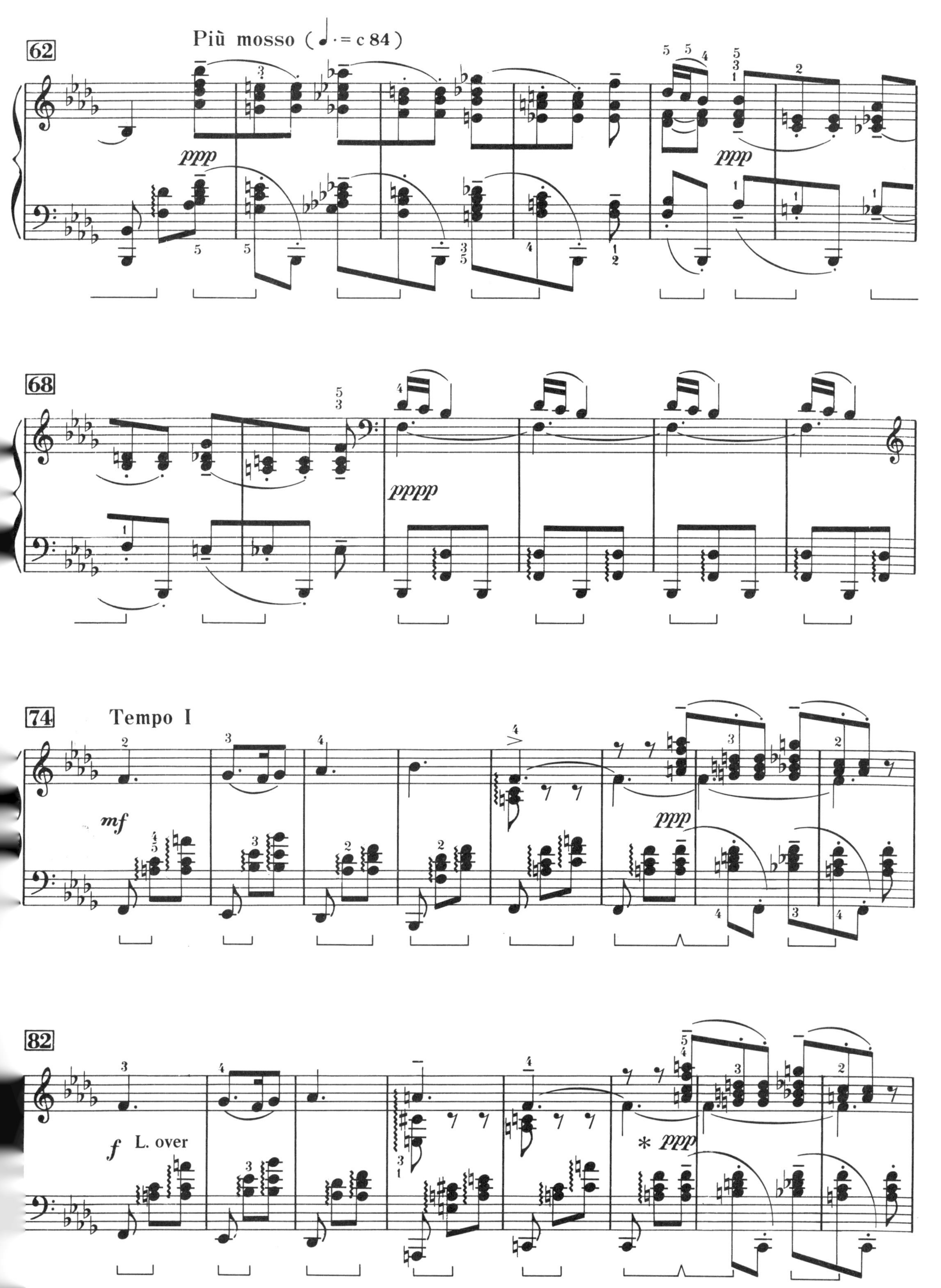

* The Siloti edition omits the downstemmed F's for the right hand in measures 88 and 89, tied from measure 87.

90
pp
ppp
98
pppp
cresc.
105
dim.
mf
p
112
118
dim.
rit.

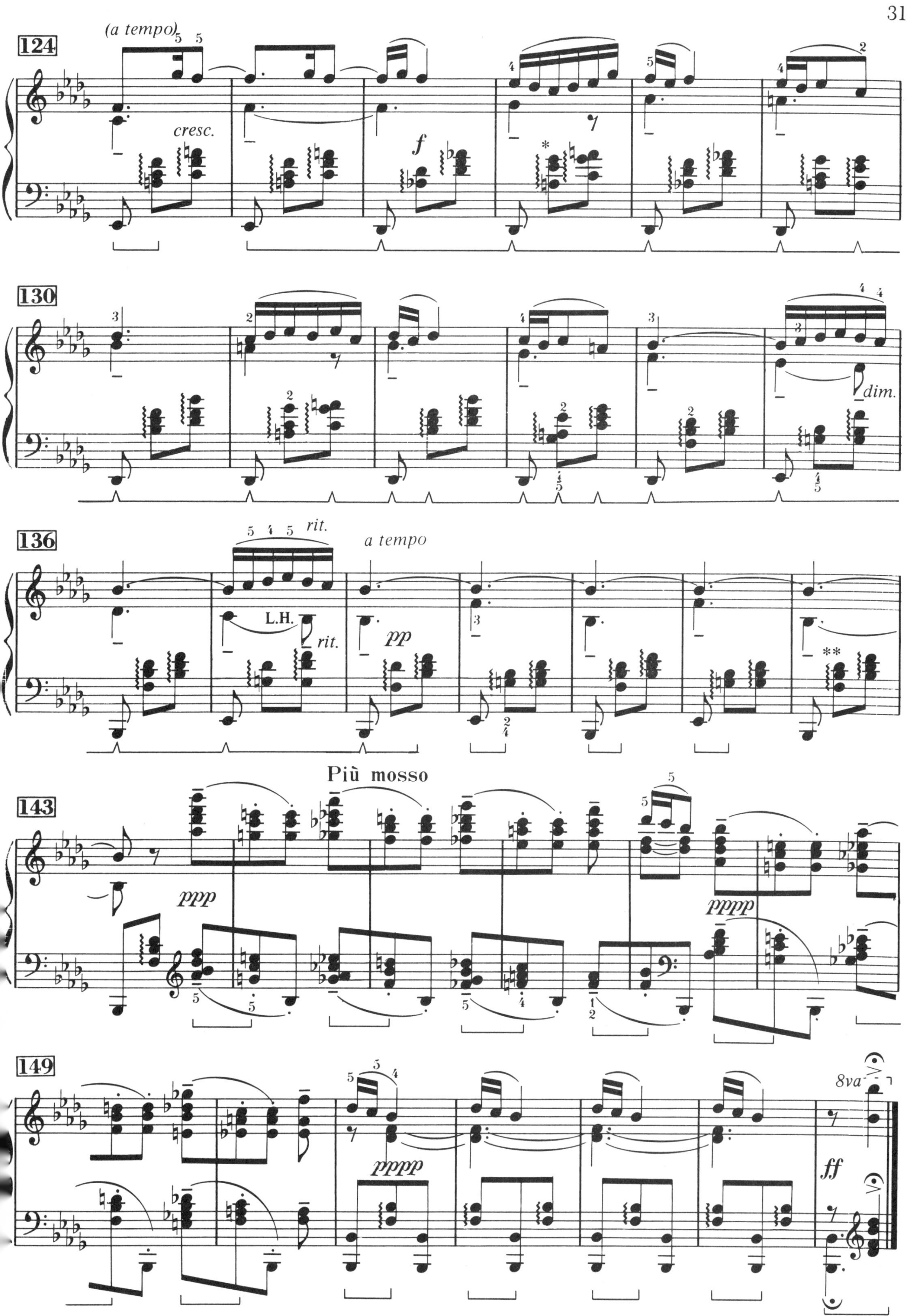

*In measure 127 Siloti omits the top G-flat of the L.H. chord on the second beat.

**In measure 142 the B-flats for the L.H. on the second and third beats are also omitted by Siloti.

BARCAROLLE in G Minor

Op. 10, No. 3
(1893)

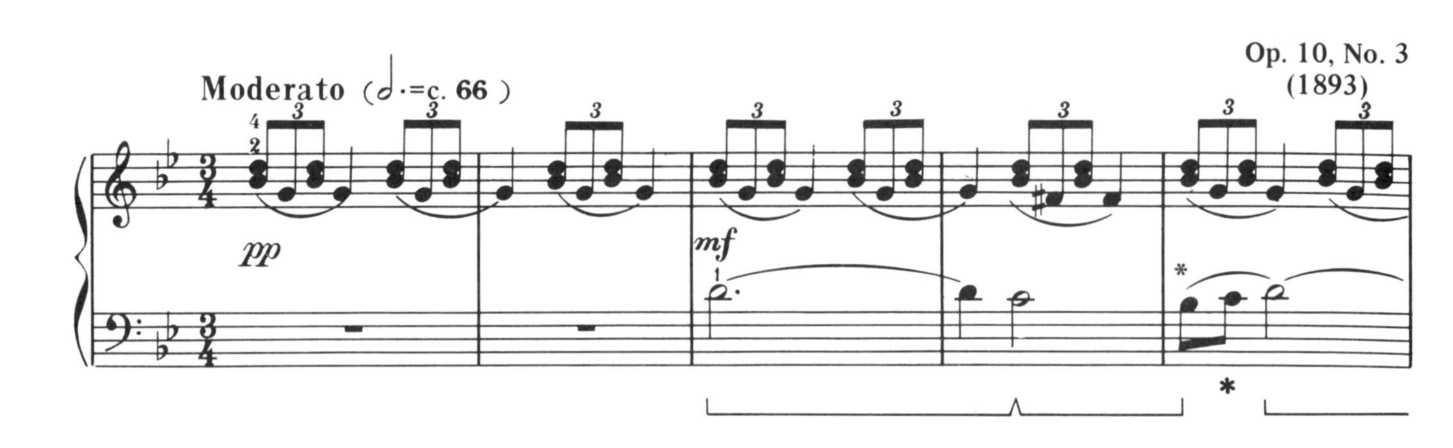

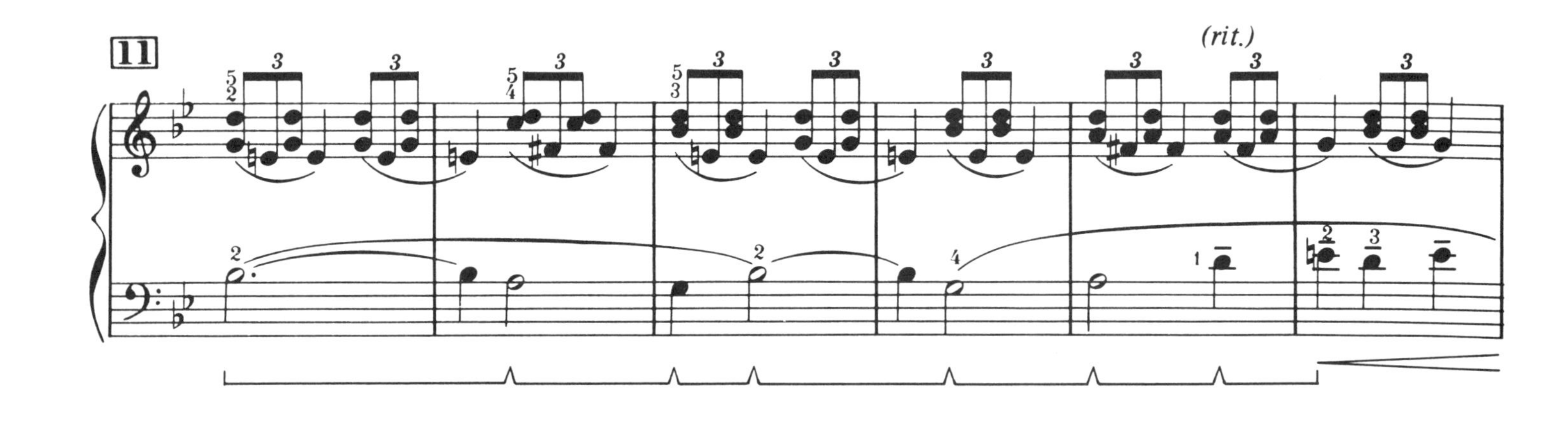

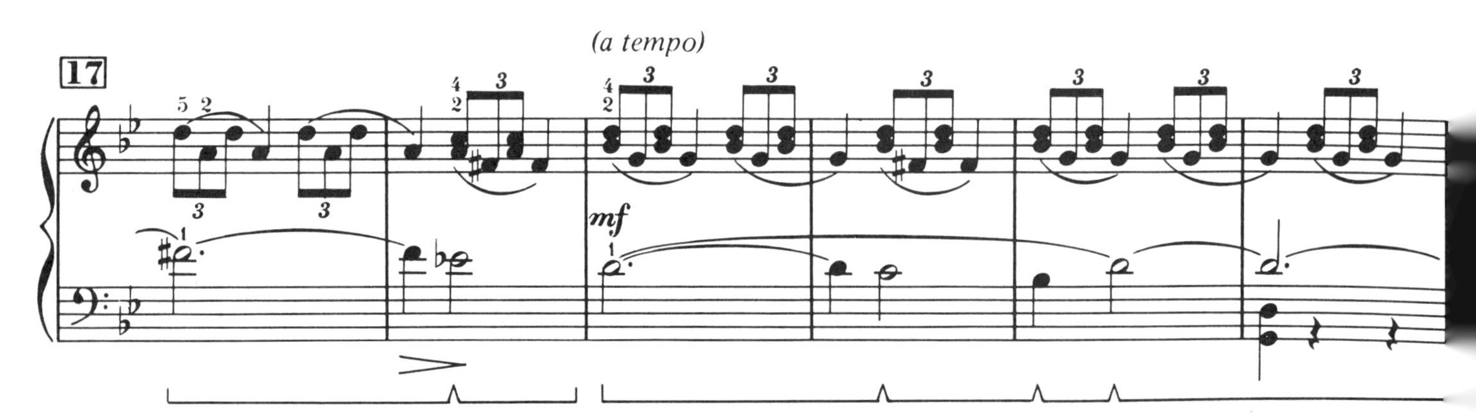

*In measure 5, and often in similar places, Rachmaninoff in a recording played a B-flat quarter note on the first beat rather than two eighths (B-flat, C) as in the printed version.

23
29
35
41
47
f
mf
pp
p

53
pp
pp
59
65
69
Con moto
ppp
leggiero
73

76
79
p
82
85
dim.
f
87

89
pp
ppp
92
95
98
f
101
f

104
107
ppp
110
Presto
pppp
113
ppp
116

* At measure 127 and similar places the problem of sustaining the bass clef D into measure 128 without blurring the harmony may be solved as indicated or by playing the D with the left hand and carefully half-pedaling measure 128.

134
137
cresc.
139
f
mf
142
145

148
mf
pp
151
153
p
156
pp
159
ppp
Meno mosso

162
165
168
171
Con moto
ppp
174

177
180
mf
183
f
ppp
186

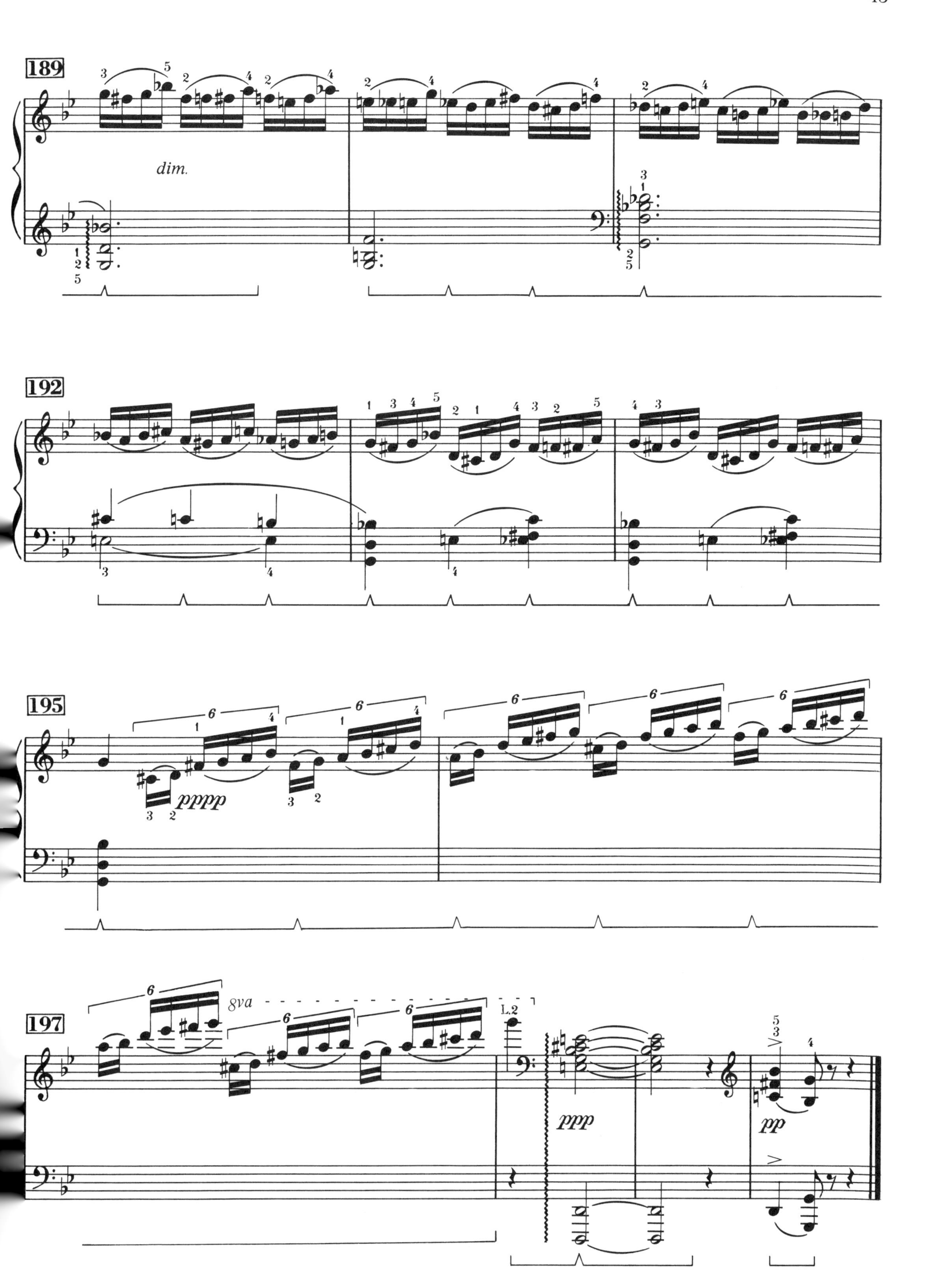
189
dim.
192
195
pppp
197
8va
L.2
ppp
pp

MÉLODIE in E Minor

Op. 10, No. 4
(1893)

28
ff
f
34
ff
mf
41
p
p
mf
pp
R.H.
48
pp

55
mf
f
dim.
p

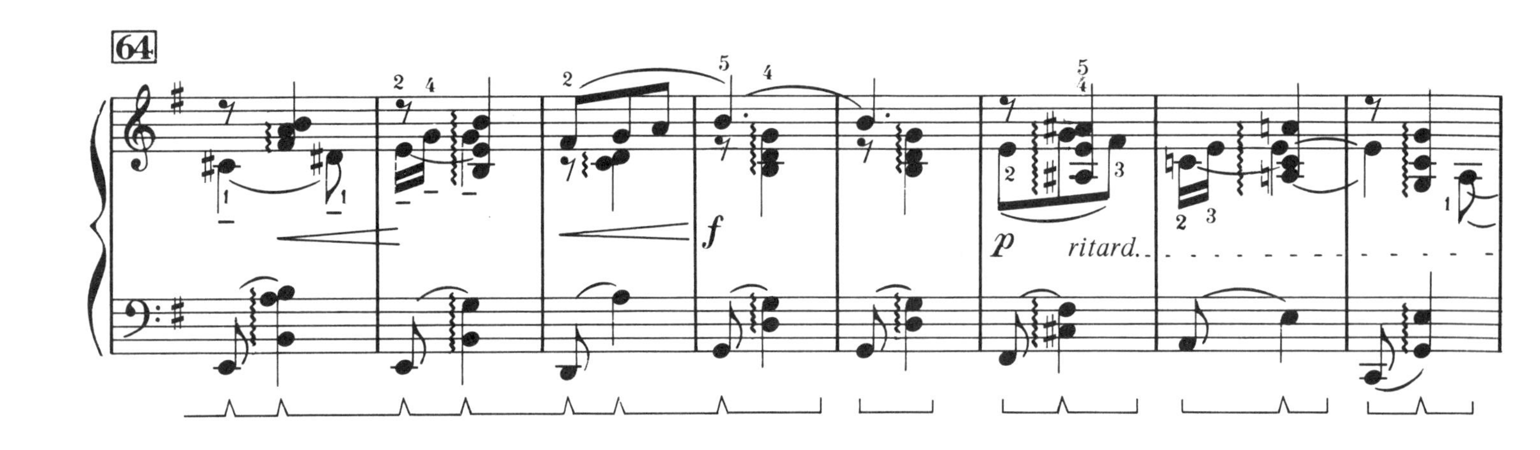
64
f
p
ritard.

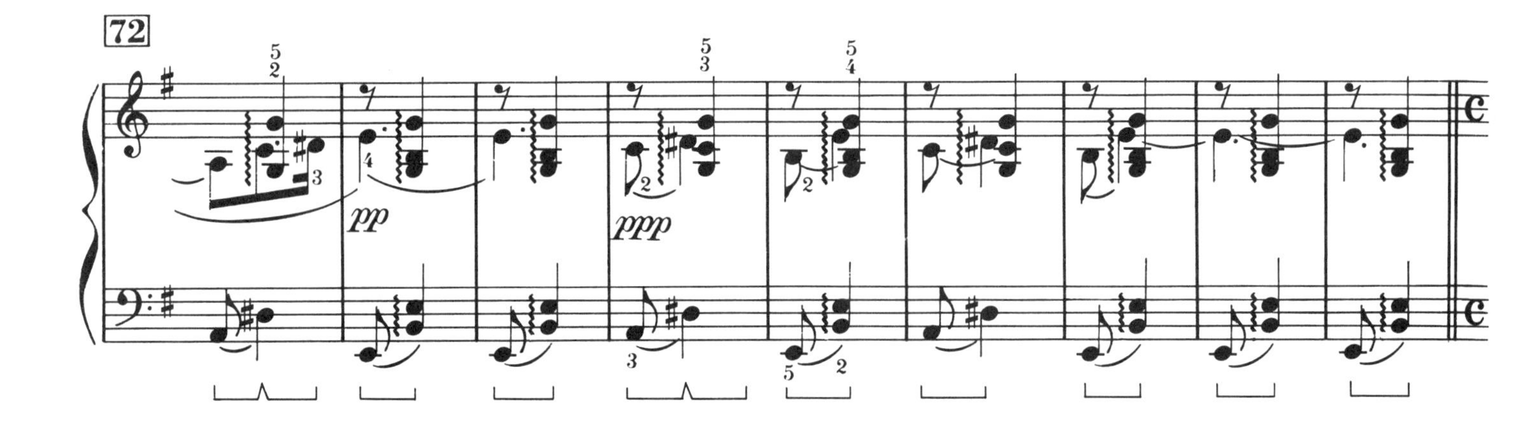
72
pp
ppp

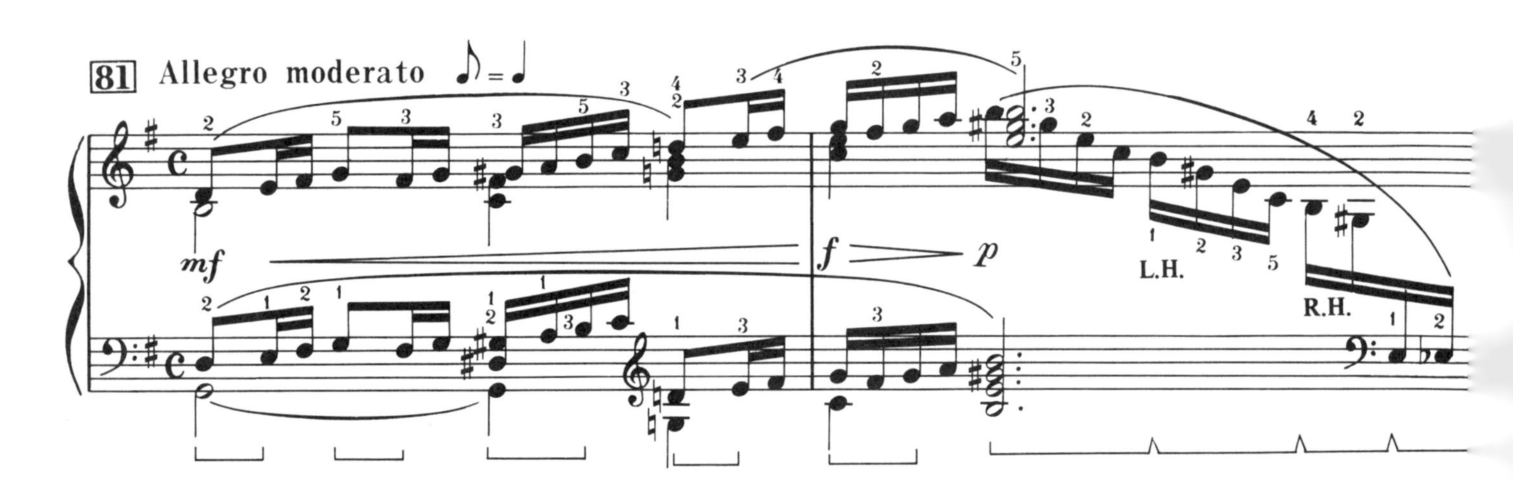
81
Allegro moderato
mf
f
p
L.H.
R.H.

83
f
L.H.
R.H.
L.H.
85
mf
p
pp
88
ppp
mf
90
f
p
L.H.
R.H.
L.H.
mf

92
L.H.
R.H.
95
ritard.
98
Allegretto
106
cresc.

115
pp
ppp
124
Moderato
mf
f
L.H.
R.H.
126
8va
129
p
rit. e dim.

HUMORESQUE in G

Op. 10, No.5
(1893)

31
pp
37
mf
43
f
49
ff
pp
56
p
f

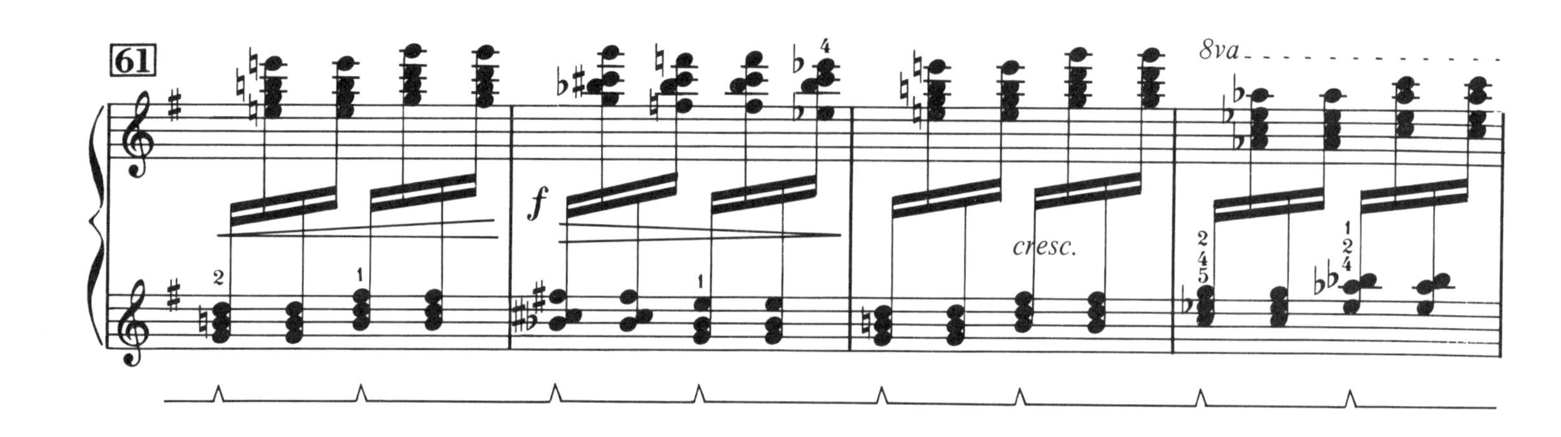
61
8va
f
cresc.

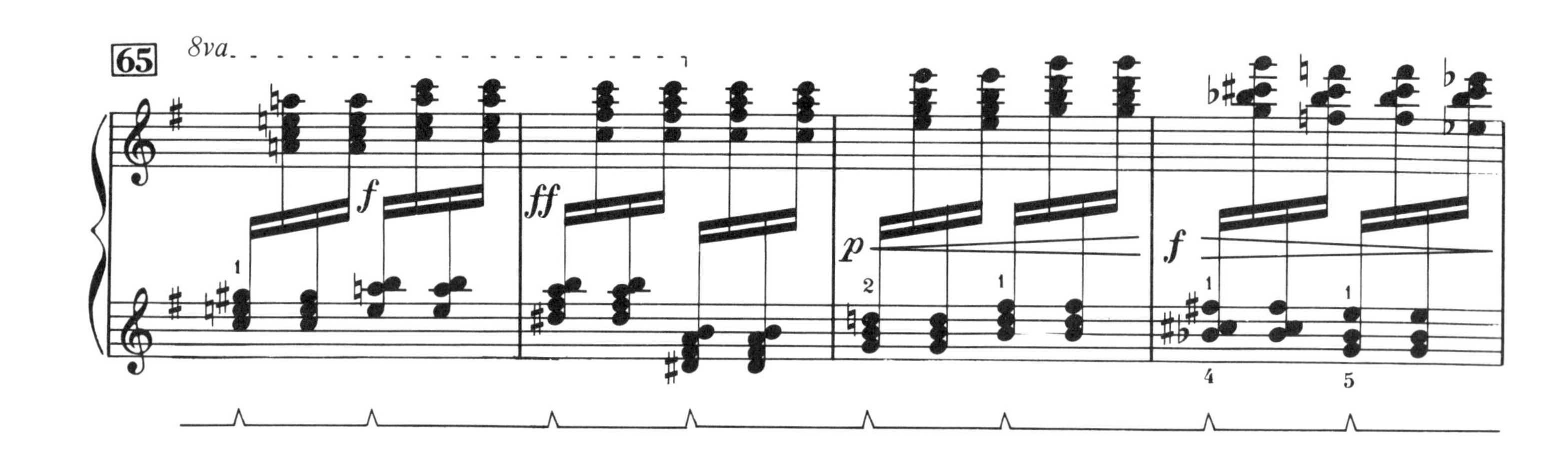
65
8va
f
ff
p
f

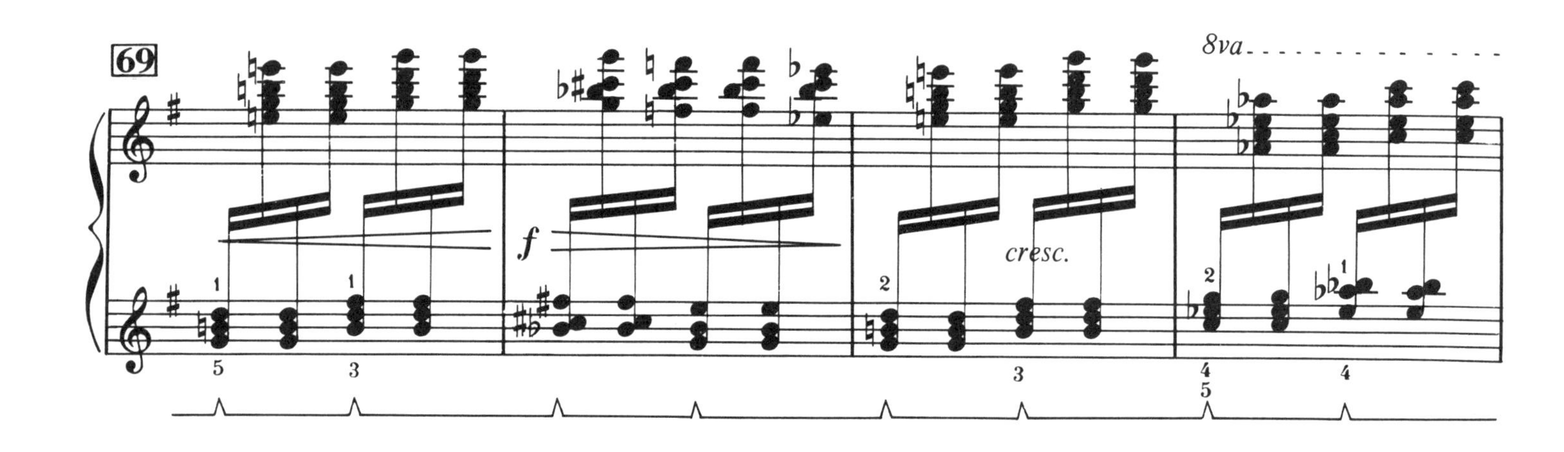
69
f
cresc.
8va

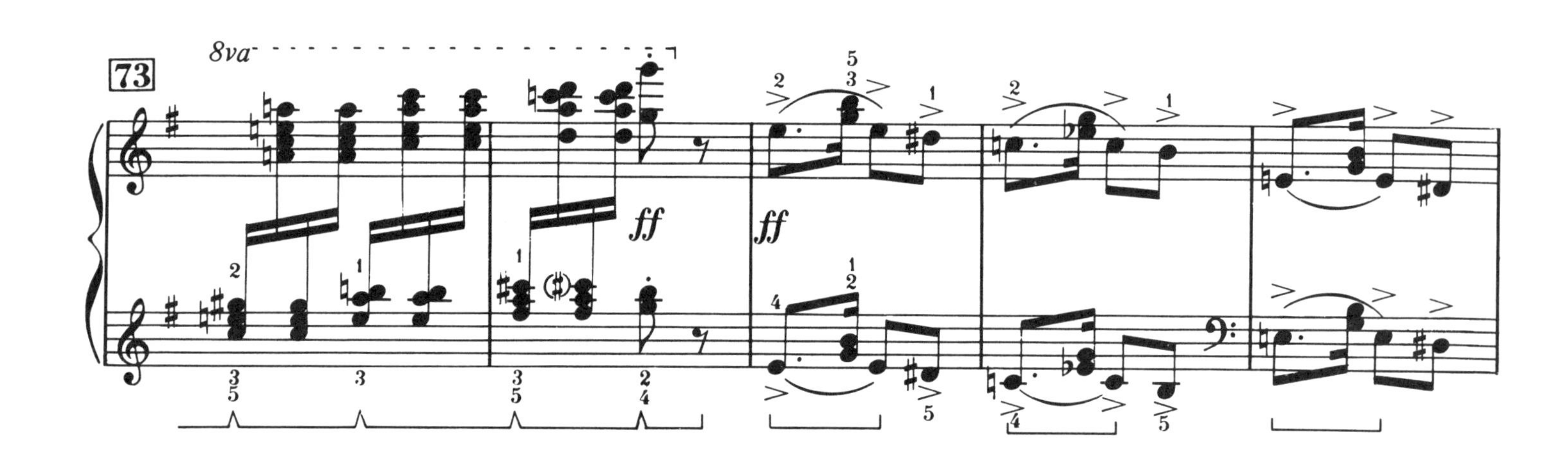
73
8va
ff
ff

*In measures 90 and 112 the composer played a C-sharp between the C and D in the right hand melody when he made the Ampico recording.

108
p
dim.
pp
114
mf
pp
pp
120
126
dim.
ppp cresc. ed accel.

133 Tempo I
f
140
ff
cresc.
147
fff con fuoco
154
8va

161
8va
ff
8va
169
8va
ppp rapido
175
pp
179
cresc.

183
dim.e rit.
pp
187
cresc.
192
p
f
p
f
196
8va
cres
cen
do

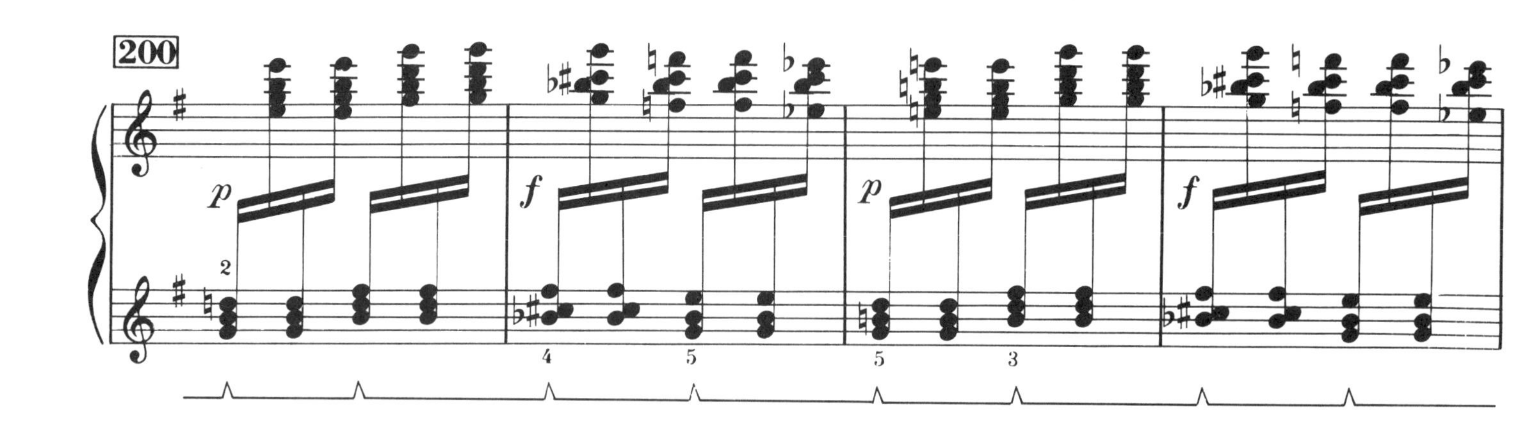
200
p
f
p
f

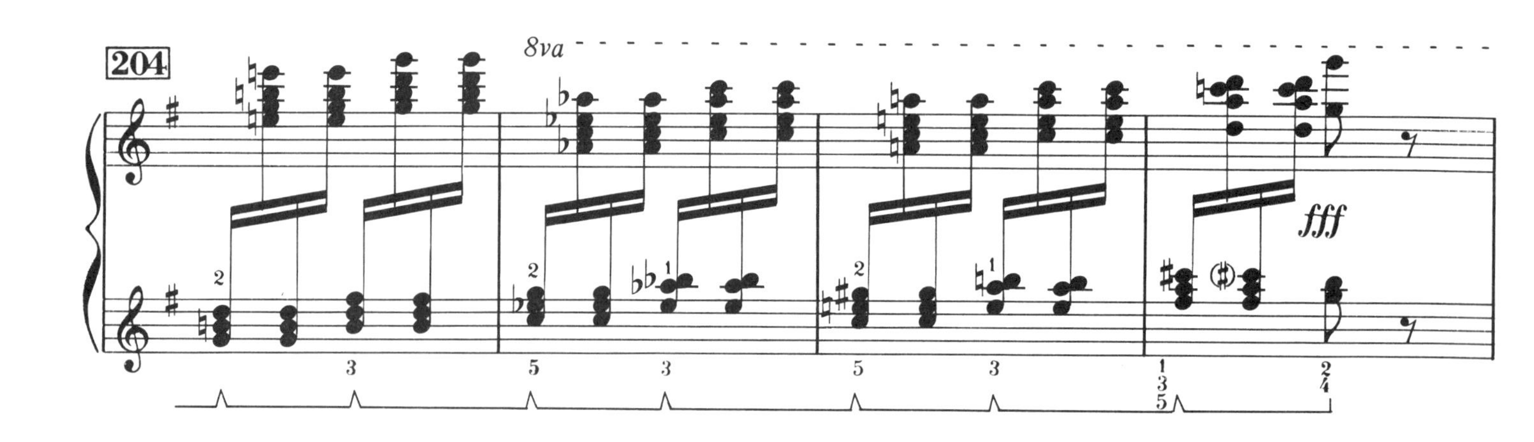
204
8va
fff

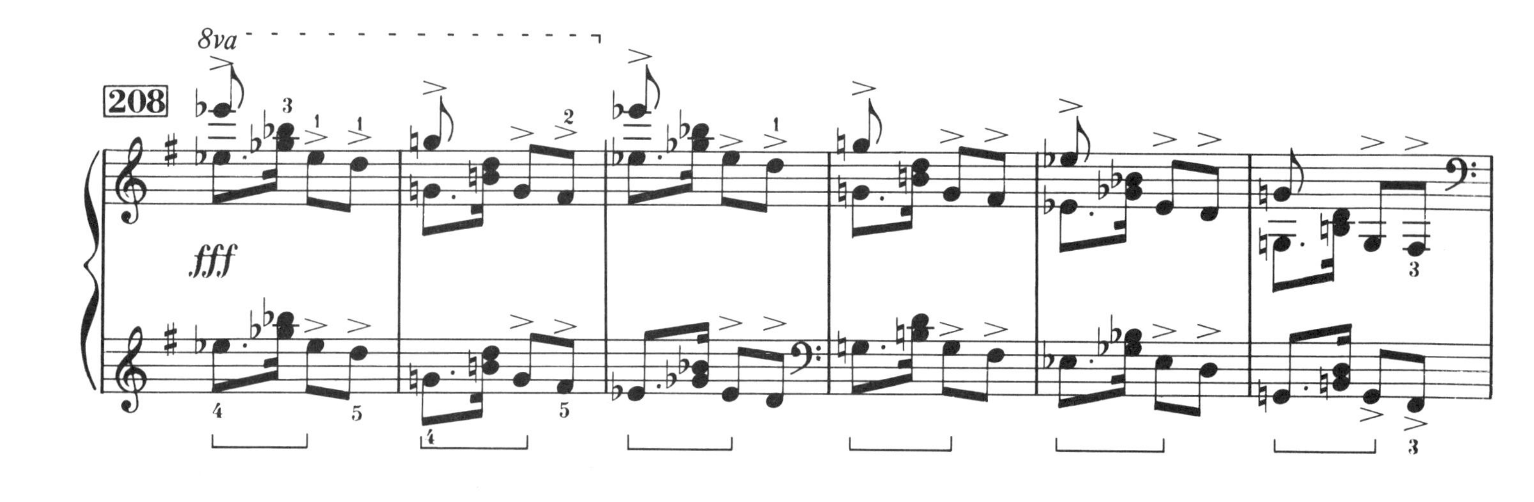
8va
208
fff

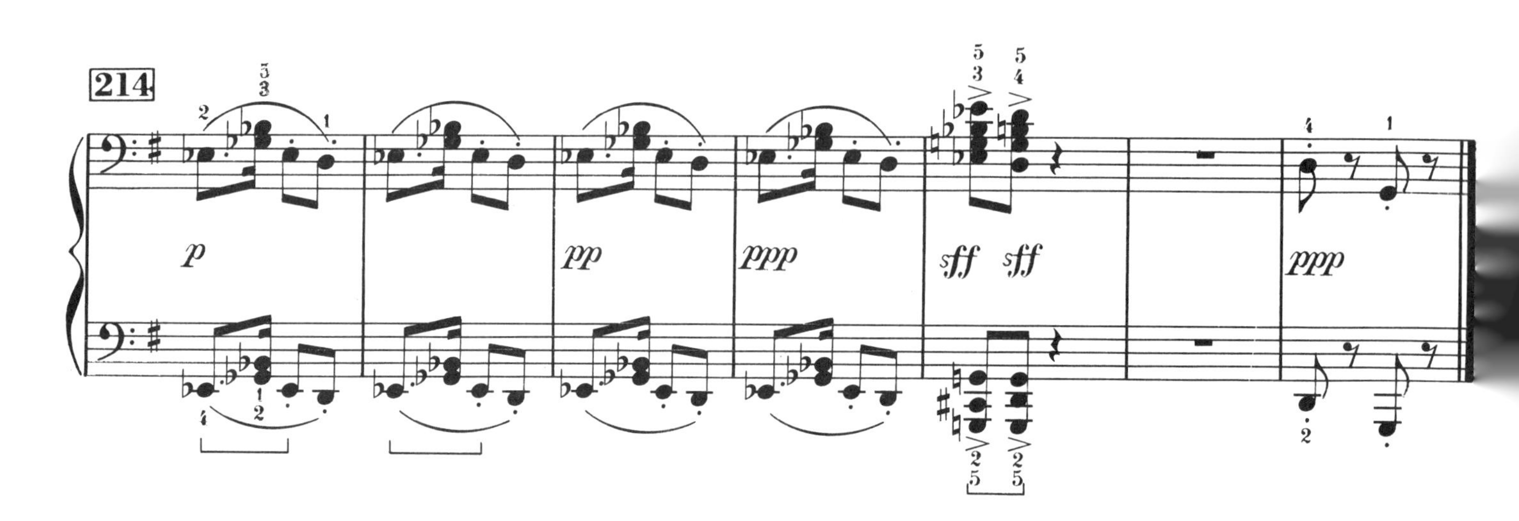
214
p
pp
ppp
sff sff
ppp

MOMENT MUSICAL in D-flat

Op. 16, No. 5
(1896)

9
dim.
p
cresc.

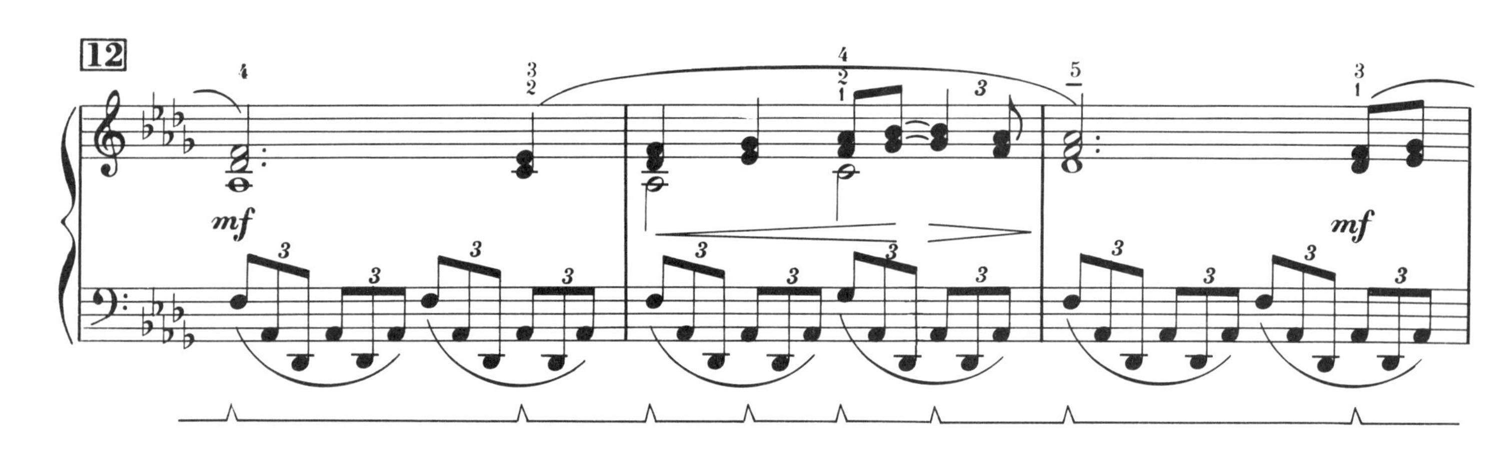
12
mf
mf

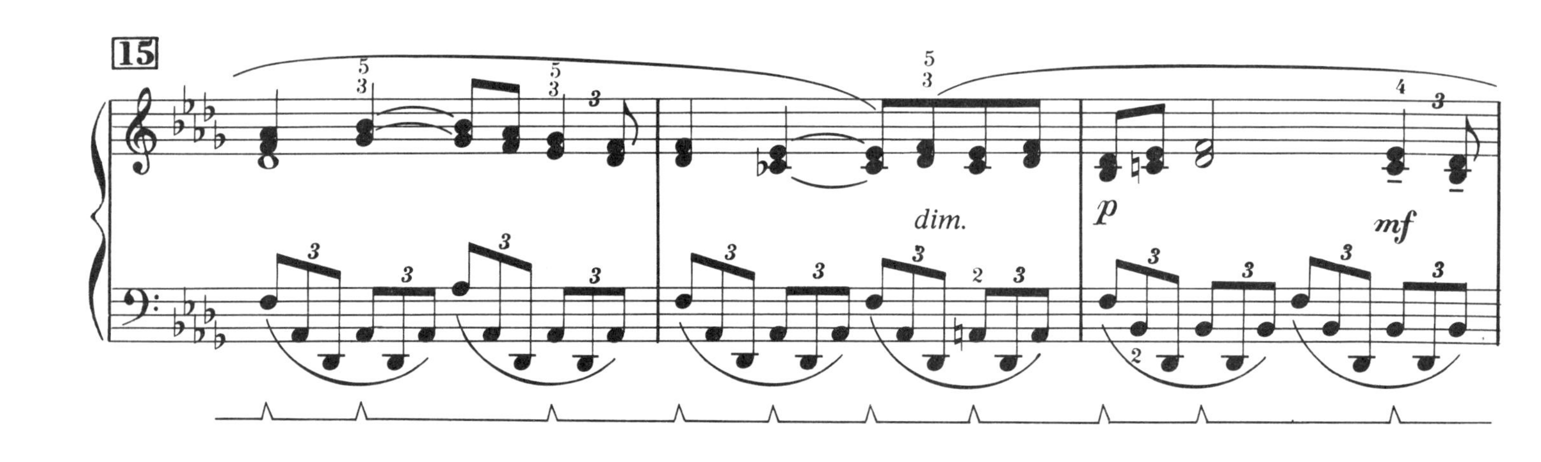
15
dim.
p
mf

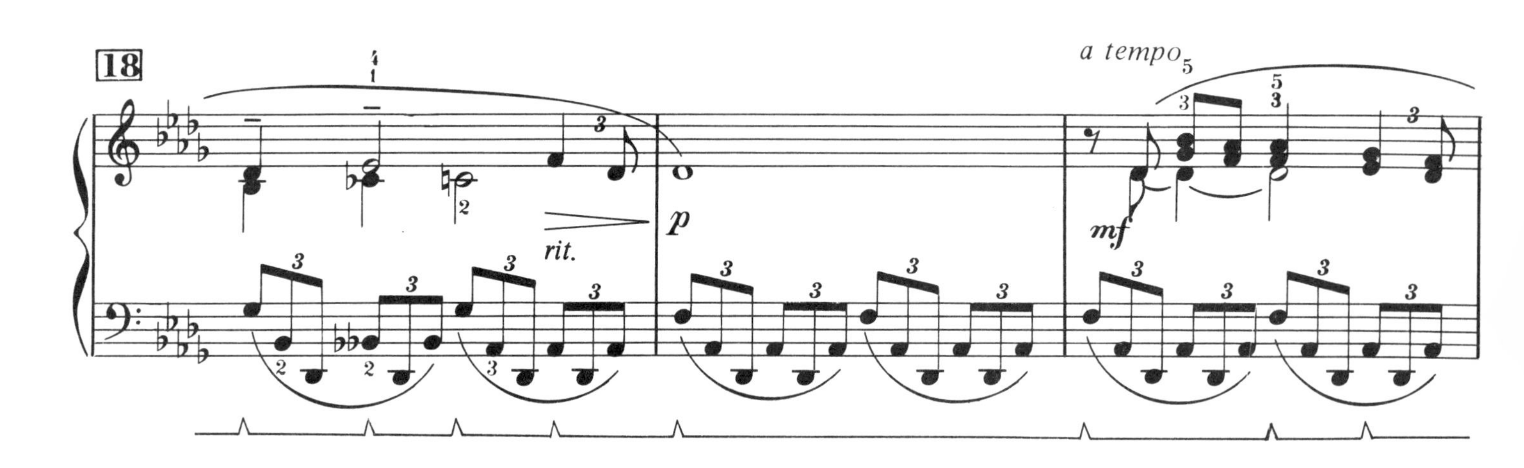
18
rit.
p
a tempo
mf

21
cresc
24
f
27
cresc.
rit.
ff
30
mf

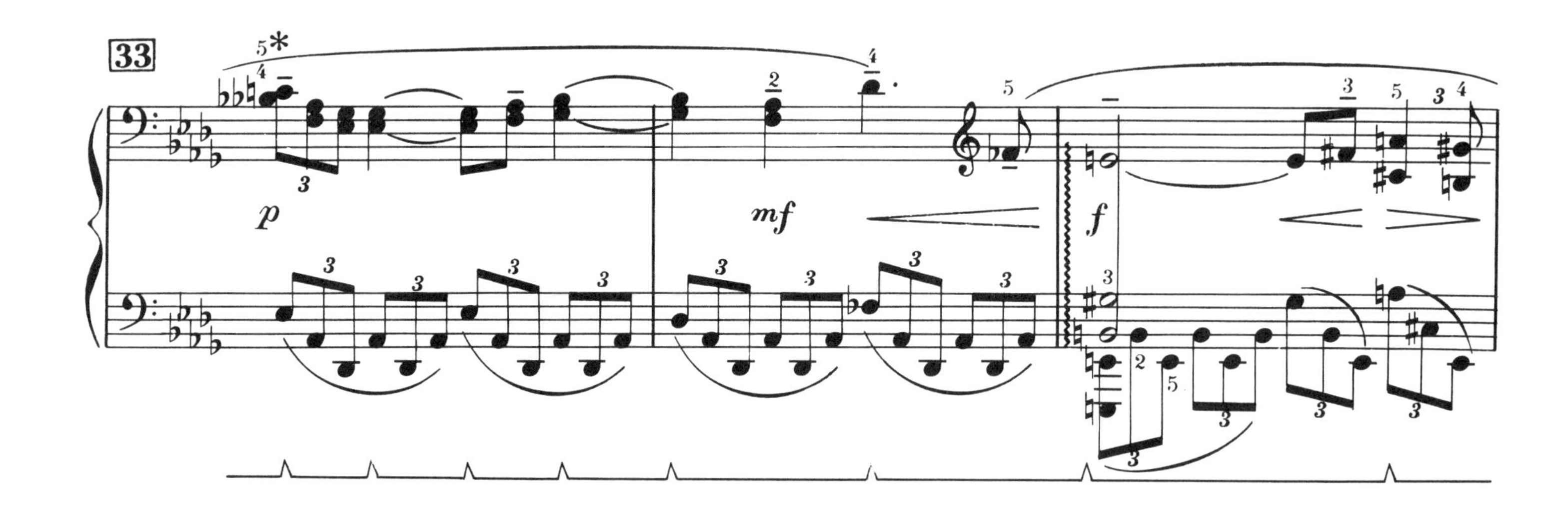

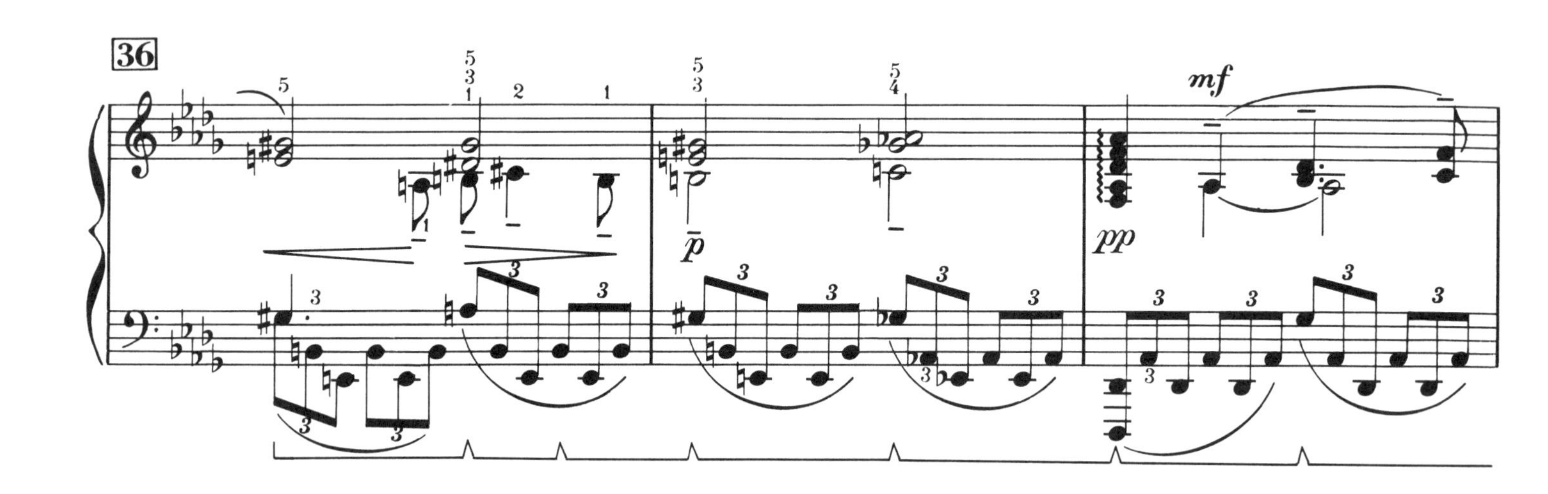

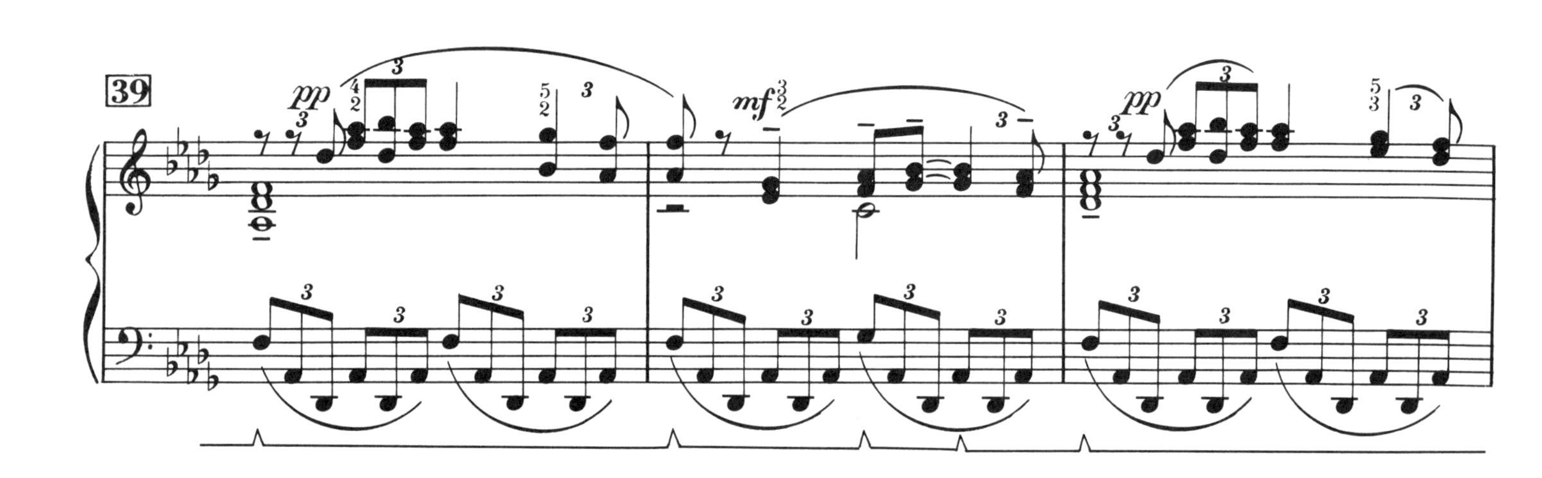

* N. B. The B-double flats played by the right hand in measure 31 and in measure 33 on this page are indicated as B-flats in some editions. Of course this makes the last right hand note in each of these measures a B-flat as well. The harmony seems less interesting with B-flats than with B double flats.

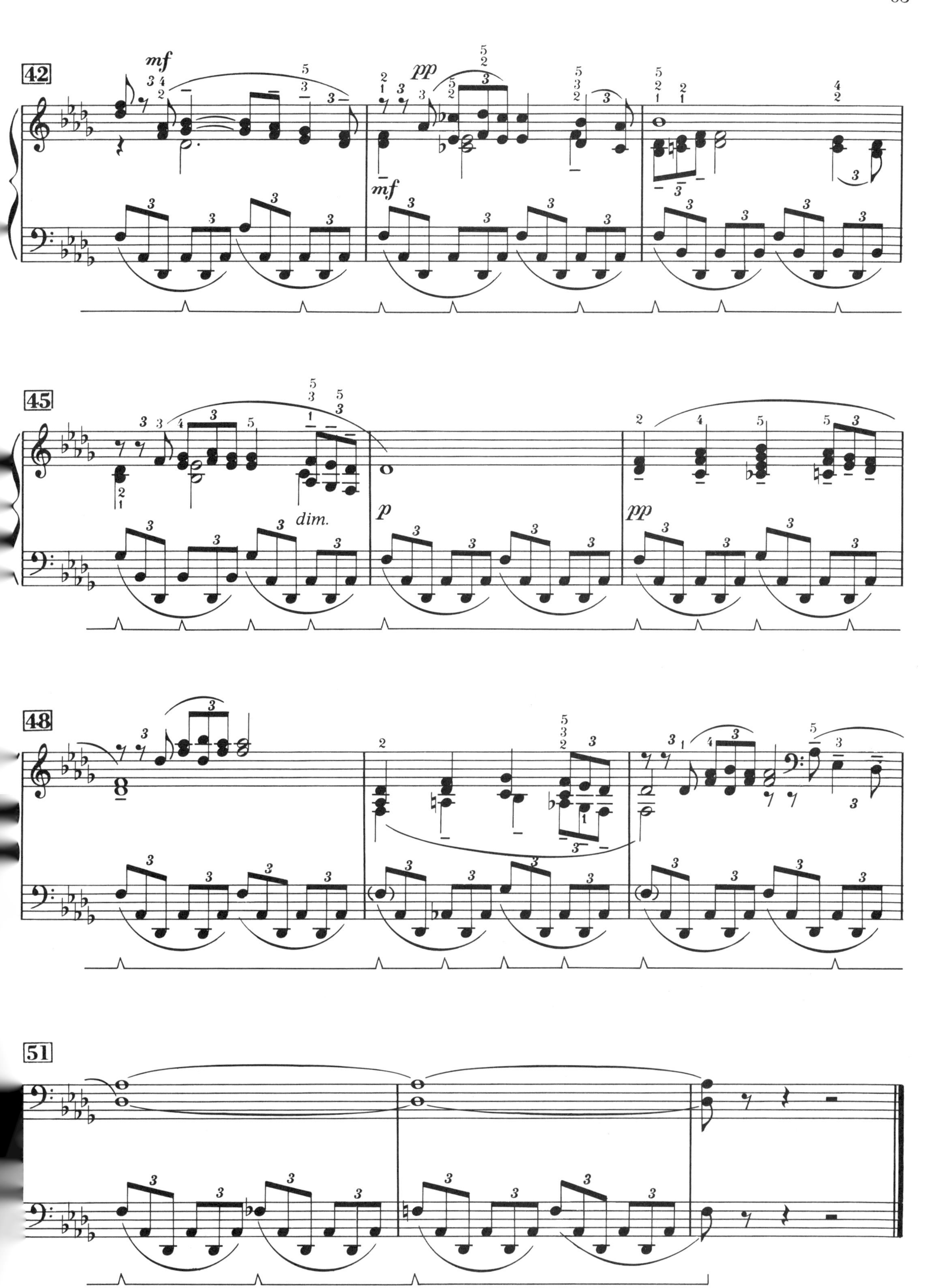

42
mf
pp
mf
45
dim.
p
pp
48
51

PRELUDE in D

Op. 23, No. 4
(1903)

14
dim.
p
f
17
p
dim.
pp
20
L.H.
24
L.H.
cresc.
f
28
dim.
mf
dim.
p

32
f
R.H.
p
dim.
R.H.
pp
36
p
mf
40
mf
rit. e dim.
a tempo
pp
44
mf
p
cresc.

48
8va
R.H.
51
8va
ff
dim.
mf
L.
55
L.
mf
58
L.
p
cresc.

61
f
L
dim.
mf
64
dim.
p
mf
L
p
68
p
p
72
dim.
pp
L.H.
mf
p
pp

PRELUDE in G Minor

Op. 23, No. 5
(1901)

13
marcato
17
20
23

26
29
dim.
32
p
dim.
Un poco meno mosso (♩ = c.76)
35
pp

37
39
cresc.
mf
41
p
43

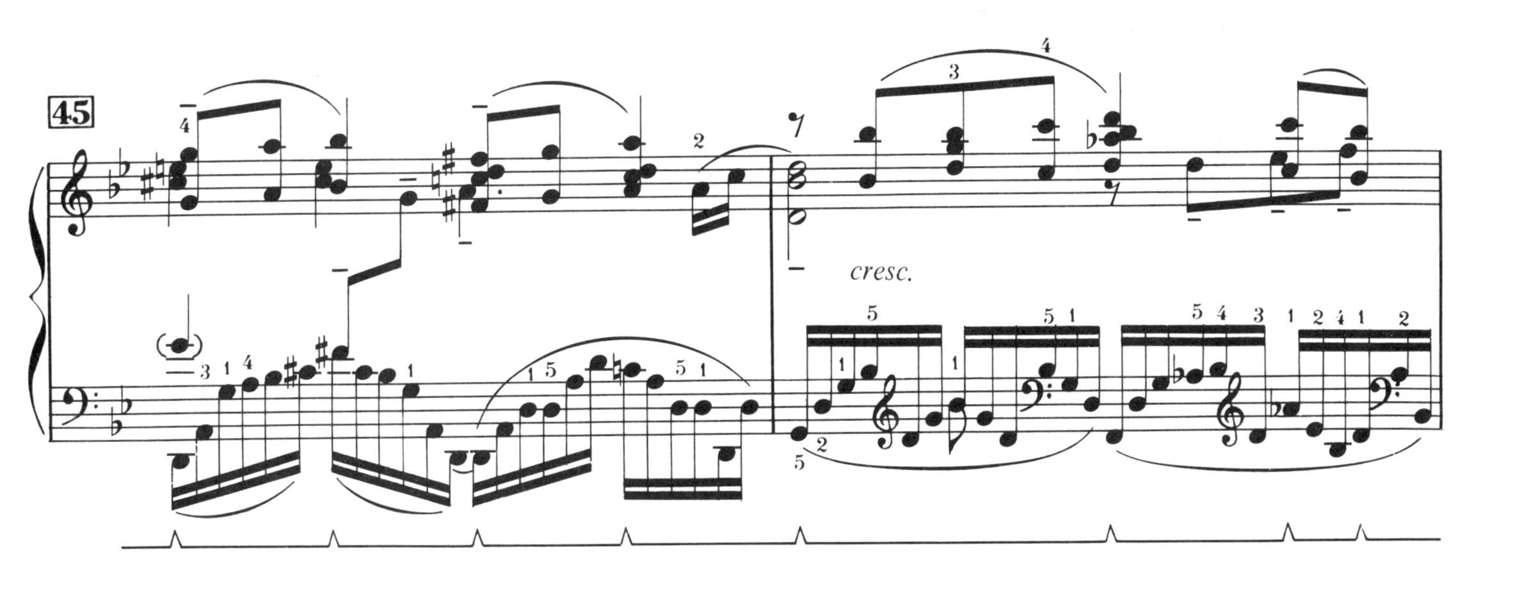
45
cresc.

47
mf
p

49
dim.e rit.
ppp

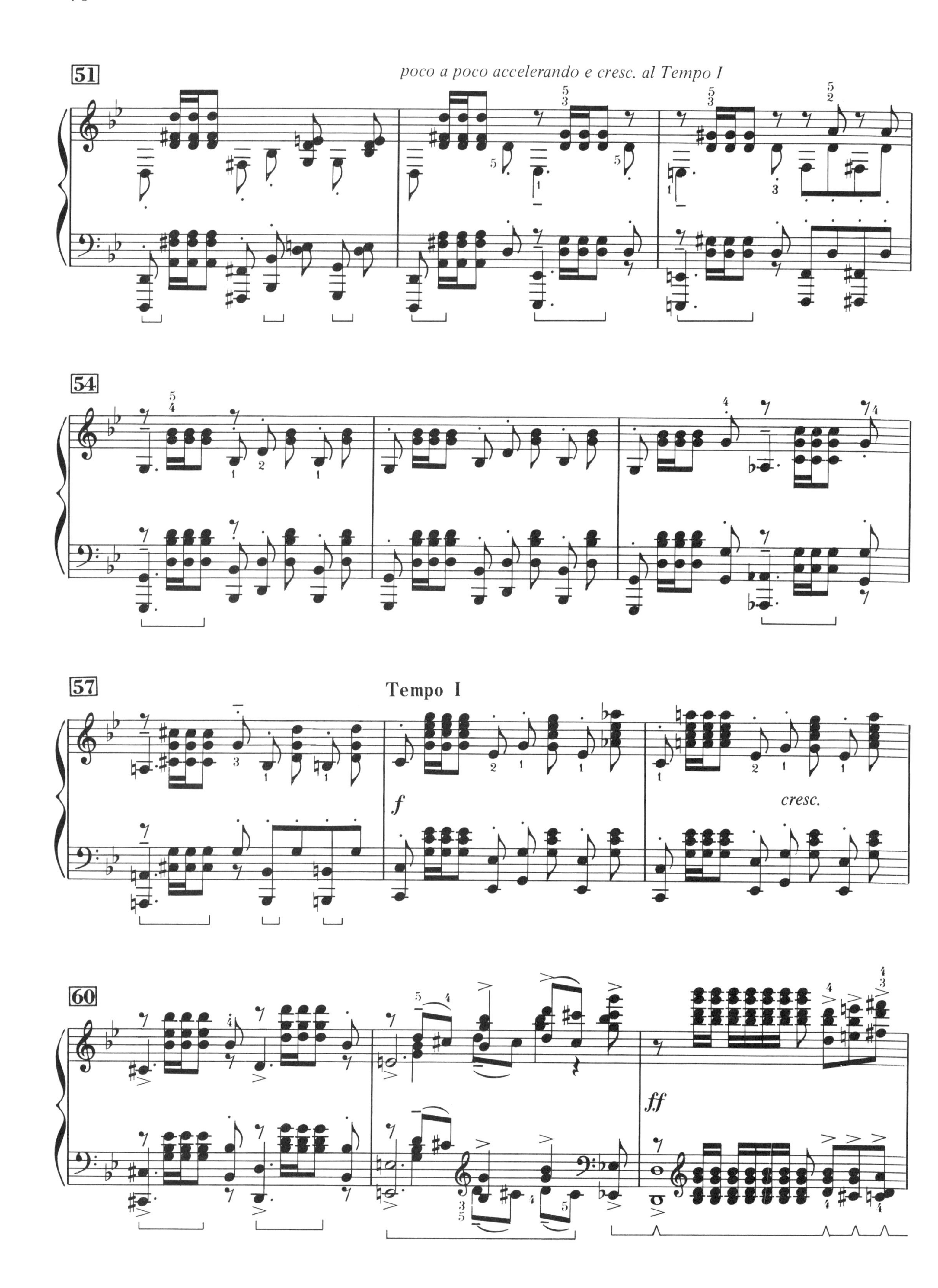
51
poco a poco accelerando e cresc. al Tempo I
54
57
Tempo I
f
cresc.
60
ff

63
f
66
69
f
ff
p
72
ff

75
78
dim.
81
p
R.H.
dim.
84
pp leggiero

PRELUDE in E-flat

Op. 23, No. 6
(1903)

p
cresc.
mf
p
p
poco a poco cresc.

17
19
8va
dim.
21
p
R
23
p
25
dim.

27
L.H.
R.H.
pp
29
R.H.
L.H.
31
R.H.
L.H.
mf
33
dim.

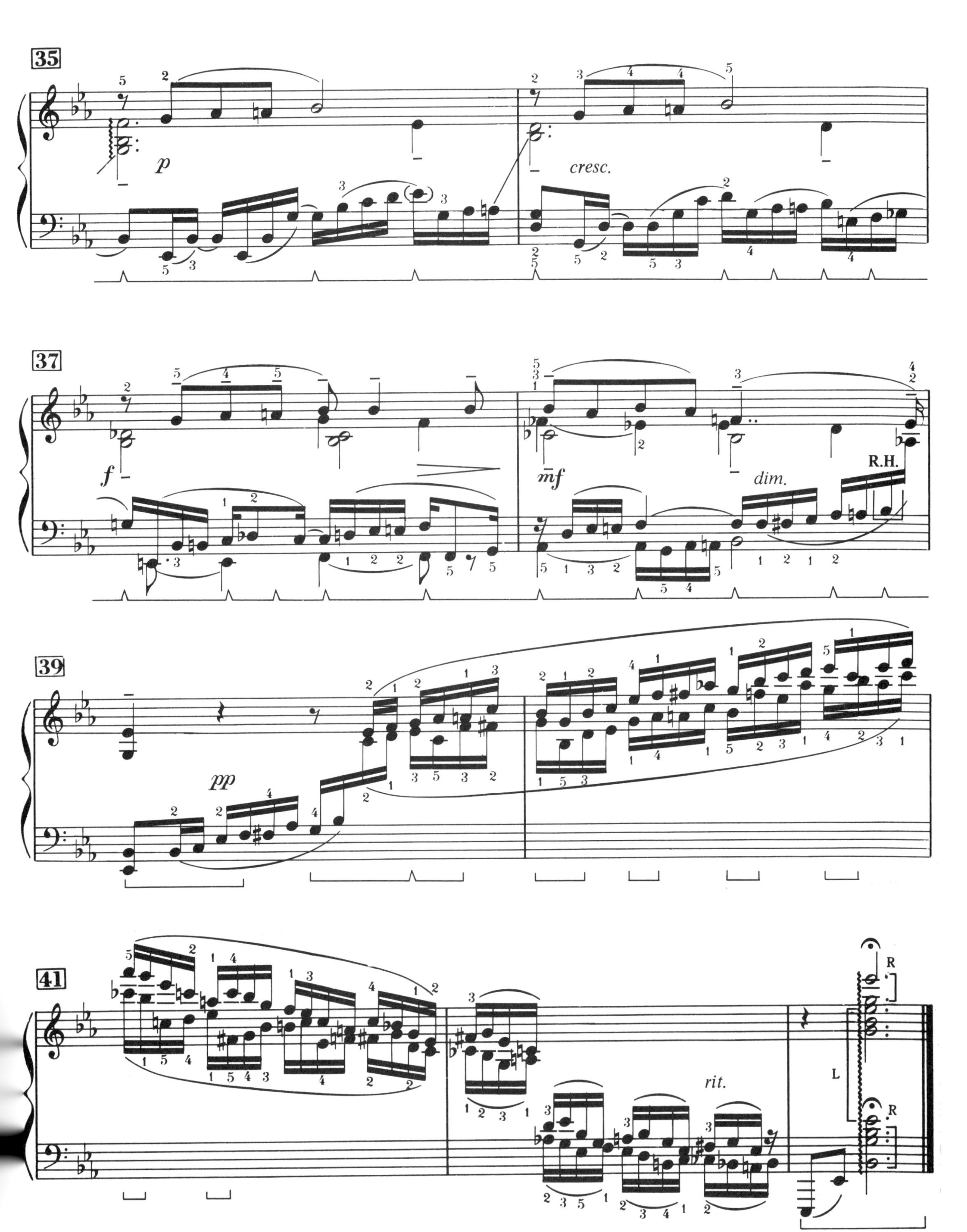

The final chord sounds beautiful if divided between the hands as indicated and played in the following rhythm:

PRELUDE in G-flat

Op. 23, No. 10
(1903)

23
ff
30
rit.
Tempo I
dim. e rit.
a tempo
dim.
p
pp
R
36
dim.
R
mf
R
cresc.
f
dim.
42
p
mf
dim. p
mf
p
pp

PRELUDE in B-flat Minor

Op. 32, No. 2
(1910)

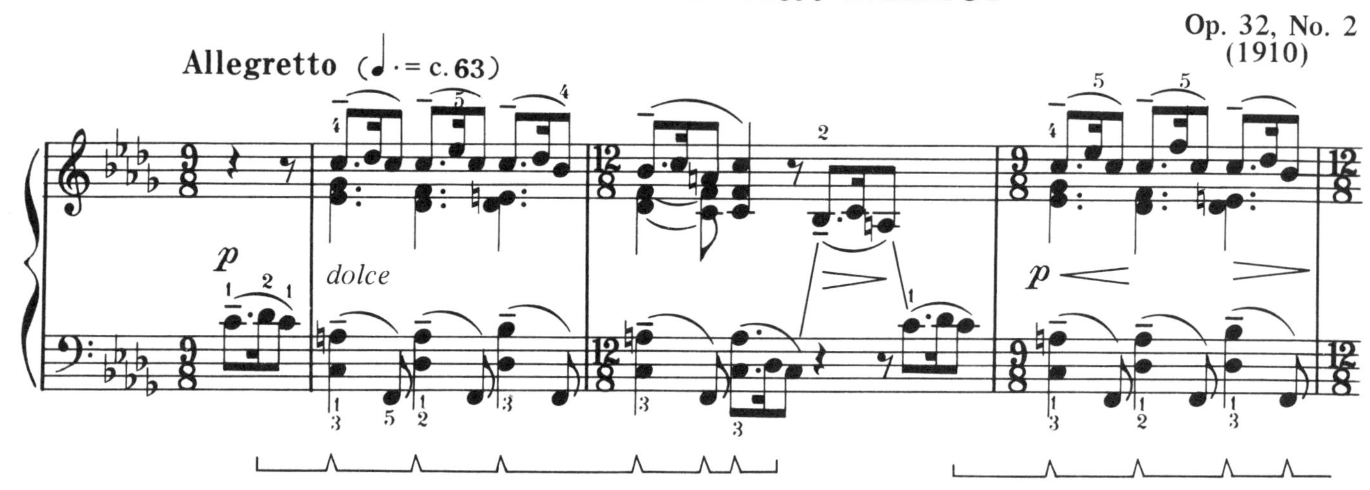

4
R.H.
mf
mf
7
un poco più mosso
pp
p
rit.
dim.
9
Tempo I
p
11
p
R.H.
pp
mf
R.H.

un poco più mosso
rit.
a tempo
R.H.
R.H.
pp
(♩. = c. 84)
pp poco a poco accel.
mf
p
poco a poco cresc.

Allegro (♩. = c. 96)
ff
dim.
mf
dim.
veloce
f
dim.
rit.

35
Meno mosso
rit.
Allegro moderato (♩. = c. 84)
mf
p
dim.
pp
38
p
40
42
mf poco a poco accel.
p
dim.

44
Allegro scherzando (♩. = c. 84)
pp
una corda
mf
dim.
tre corde
46
p
f
dim.
p
49
f
mf
52
dim.
perdendo
p
dim.
pp

PRELUDE in G

Op. 32, No. 5
(1910)

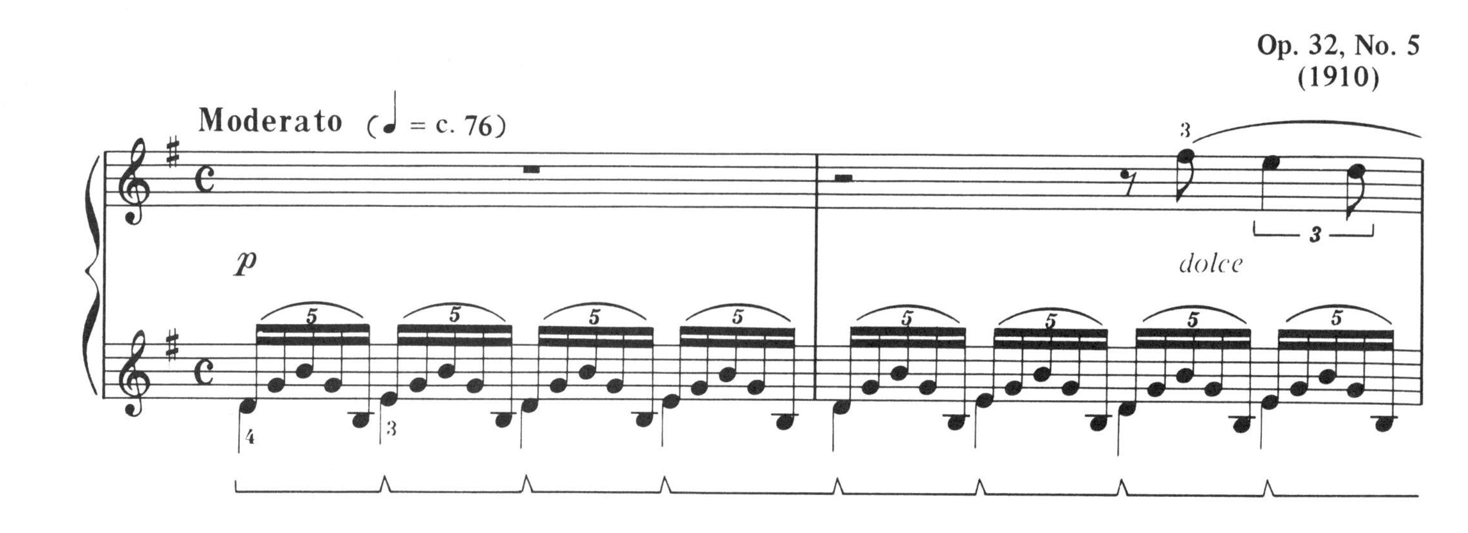

7
pp
dim.
9
ppp
pp
p
tre corde
11
rit.
13
a tempo
dim.
pp

15
17
p
19
pp
21
veloce

23
perdendo
dolce
26
dim.
dim.
28
rit.
a tempo
dim.
30

32
pp
34
p
pp leggiero
36
p
38
perdendo
pp

PRELUDE in F

(a) (o) = Depress this key silently and hold through the measure in order to sustain the low F.

13
dim.
pp
16
rit.
a tempo
dim.
pp
p
19
Più vivo
poco
a poco cresc.
22

f
ff
dim.
p
dim.
pp
rit.
pp

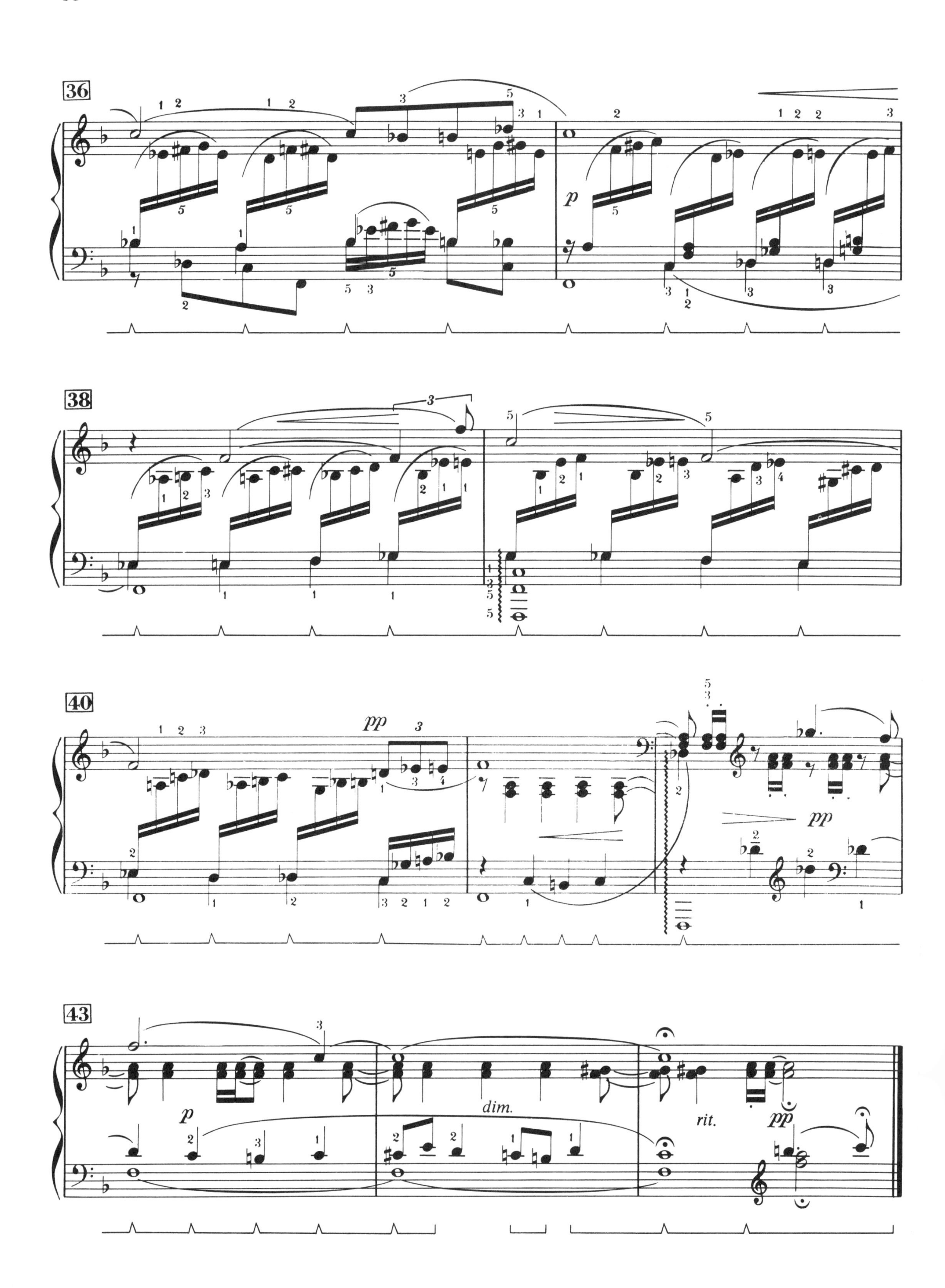
36
p
38
40
pp
43
p
dim.
rit.
pp

PRELUDE in B Minor

Op. 32, No. 10
(1910)

16
pp
mf
pesante
19
poco a poco cresc.
rit.
22
Tempo I
ff
25
28
ff

ff
dim.
f
rit. e dim.
L'istesso tempo
pp
poco cresc.
dim.
p
poco cresc.

42
leggiero
mf
dim.
44
pp
cresc.
46
f
dim.
48
p veloce

48
8va
L.H.
dim.
pp
mf
49
a tempo, come prima
mf
53
dim.
57
mf
p
pp

PRELUDE in B

Op. 32, No. 11
(1910)

26
rit.
a tempo
p
dim.
pp
33
p
mf
40
dim.
p
rit.
a tempo
pp
48
pp
p
pp

54
pp
p
59
pp
mf
f
mf
64
rit.
a tempo
dim.
p
pp
70
pp
mf
dim.
p

76
p
pp
p
81
rit.
a tempo
mf
p
87
pp
mf
93
pp
p
rit.
ppp
pp
una corda

ETUDE-TABLEAU in G Minor

Op. 33, No. 8
(1911)

10
p
mf
12
dim.
p
mf
14
p
mf
cresc.
f
7
pp
mf

poco rit.
dim.
pp
veloce
cresc.
L.H.
f
L.H.
ff

29
rit.
30
ff
mf
32
8va
pp
f
p
pp
36
Tempo I
pp
R
mf
p
mf

38
dim.
p
mf
40
p
mf
p
cresc.
poco accel.
42
43
ff
sff
pp